first, you swallow the moon

a novel of heartbreak and wilderness by kipp wessel

FIRST, YOU SWALLOW THE MOON

Published by

 radialGRAIN

www.radialGRAIN.com

First Edition

Published in the United States of America
ISBN 978-0-9909248-0-7
Cover design by Ted Crandall, *2 Cat Design*
Author photograph by Britt Nicole Wessel

for my brothers

Kerrik and Kemper

prologue

M OSTLY, I REMEMBER HOW PRETTY it was.

The snow sifted through crossing branches of pine and tamarack. It lit against their needles in a gentle, endless hiss.

That's the image that remains — snow combing the woods my final trek through them. The wet flakes poured from the blue mouth of storm and skimmed the bruised fingers of clouds. Their sprawling, wet bodies gained form, fused, collided against cold and one another. They shaped leaf-like spicules across their wandering descent through sky, through trees, through branches.

It was beautiful. I walked through it slowly. My breath formed ghosts. I knew I'd miss every last pocket of the varied landscape surrounding me. Through the clouds, the moon and stars swam. For a moment, that's all my world was — just snow, just stars, just breathing.

Two years earlier, I entered these woods for the first time. I approached them less from the desire to discover something new, but more out of the need to avoid something else. Each balsam and poplar I passed extended the distance from the young woman I was still in love with, separated us from the word "goodbye," each tree another finger pressed over our lips.

Part sanctuary, part world unhinged, this was the same stretch of wood I would come face to face with giants. Their heartbeats drummed through shadows. Their claws welted wide trunks of trees. They overturned boulders, huffed and thundered through meadows with gold sun pressed against their humped shoulders.

You sift through the rubble of the most wounded chapter of your life, your broken-skinned fall from grace, and you vie to recover one a lasting consolation. It becomes the final thing you barter to sustain. Despite everything else that falls into pieces at your feet or spirals from your fingertips, if you can salvage a single virtue, any emolument from the muddled history of your greatest heartbreak, maybe then you can heal. Or move forward. Or, at least – move. If your trembling fingers can wrap themselves firmly, permanently around a single, beautiful reward, maybe you can loosen your futile grip on the stars peeling across the dark, curved sea.

Even from our worst disasters, we need vestiges. Thank fucking god for the bears.

part one

We roar all like bears, and mourn sore like doves: we look for judgment, but there is none; for salvation, but it is far off from us.

Isaiah 59:11

Exit, pursued by a bear.

(Stage direction from The Winter's Tale by William Shakespeare, 1623)

Minnesota

I T BEGAN WITH HER LIPS. I imagined them pressed against mine — and mine against hers — soft, wet, and their slow movement as they formed words of introduction.

Maybe that's the way all great loves begin. Suspended — in wonder.

The first time I saw her, Clare's cheeks were red from the cold, flush from her entrance into the warm apartment. Her eyes were pretty and green.

It was a Christmas party. The windows were frosted along the edges. She wore a peach-colored sweatshirt, worn inside out, jeans, and an oversized pea coat.

"I brought the dip!" she said, and then shot the friend with whom she shared an entrance a look, and added, "I didn't mean you."

Her remark earned a laugh from those gathered nearby, deepened her blush, and she set a red Pyrex bowl of cellophane-covered artichoke dip on the table. She pulled the cellophane, bunched it in her hand and looked in my direction. Her face beamed. Our eyes met, and we both looked away.

Clare was seventeen years old – nearly three years younger than I. I had no valid memory of meeting her, but when I saw her I had this feeling we had. It was one of those moments you meet someone for the first time, or see her across a room and feel an immediate and simultaneous combination of intensely familiar and remotely known.

The two of us moved from room to room. We caught each other's glances. "Who is that girl?" I asked a friend.

"Clare Daupin. Friends with Beth and Sara. She's nice."

For the remainder of the night, my concentration moved from intermittent conversations, to the open bottles of wine, to snow falling through the window, to Clare. Mostly to Clare.

I spent the evening wanting to talk with her. She would later confirm the desire was mutual. But we didn't talk. We didn't meet, not until the end of the evening when she was descending the stairs, preparing to leave. I had watched her pull her coat across her chest, wrap her scarf around her neck, murmur a final few smiling good-byes and disappear through the door frame when a rush of adrenaline pushed me through the crowded apartment, past the doorway, and down the stairs.

The heavy oak and glass entrance door clicked into its frame, and Clare stood on the other side of the frosted glass, a labyrinth of curb-parked cars and sidewalk snow banks behind her. And then she glanced over her shoulder. My heart thudded. My mouth parted, but failed to find voice. Not a single word.

I smiled at my own muteness and the closed door between us.

Clare smiled back. She waited a moment and reached toward the glass. She drew her gloved finger across the pane and shaped seven beautiful numerals, the first three and then the final four, separated by a dash.

Never in my life would I pray as intensely, in an isolated moment, for the skill of memorization.

She opened her hand and closed it in a wave. And then she walked away. From that moment, nothing was ever the same. The sea of my life parted. Over the next three years, we became inseparable, our bodies and lives seamlessly joined. Until my brother's awful death changed everything again.

The moon is full – obese – ripe enough to burst wide open. Dark branches stretch across its face and blue their bark. The sloping trail beneath them – moon and trees – is riddled with wet prints across soil, the shapes of rounded stars.

Following my brother's death, I dreamt the world through the eyes of bears. I'm not sure why. Maybe it was because my brother was a force of nature, not unlike a bear. When Ben stormed into our house, the entire structure – joists and rafters, trembled. Or maybe the connective tissue between my bear dreams and my brother's death stemmed from a singular memory, one buried in the granular shoal of our early life experience. We were five and nine. Ben and I were tromping through the woods behind our house, rooting through the leaf mold for banded woolly caterpillars. We lifted their weightless bodies, curled like furry macaroons, set them down on drier mulch, and tucked them back into their leafy beds.

It was late autumn. Brittle oak and maple leaves skittered across the path in front of our small feet. We could see our breath.

And then the yearling – a black bear so close to my own size I mistook him as a potential schoolmate when his form interspersed the trees. He bounded through the crimson sumac. Red leaves swirled behind him, and he launched his body onto a two-foot wide oak. His rear claws scratched loose small shreds of bark on his hastened ascent. He pulled himself to the first limb, wrapped his front paws around it and stared at us – the bear and two humans wordlessly dumbfounded by one another's existence.

Nothing happened. And then Ben reached for my shoulder and pulled me into his chest. He cupped my chin in his in the crook of his arm – my big brother, my protector.

"Don't move," he said. "Not an inch."

All these years later, with Ben gone, that bear, or bears like it, reappeared. They showed in droves – not in the woods behind our house, but in the wide acreage of my dreams. And in those dreams, I gradually but assuredly became one of them.

I fell between salty waves of sleep and imagined moonlight through bogs, my breath salmon blood and berry sugar, my footprints in the cold mud five-toed stars. The world, the tree line and marl, was steeped in moonlight and musky reed grass, marsh fern, and prairie star, the cold boreal heart of the montane, the mineral soils of the talus. I roamed the same woods they did, through long crossing shadows of hemlock and cedar, my dreamt footsteps alongside theirs in the dewed soil.

Weeks following my family's vigil alongside Ben's hospital bed, I sensed a small, remote opening within my chest transforming, cell by cell, a newly birthed muscle gathering what it could of calm.

And then the chambers of my heart felt as though they had doubled their size. Their single clutches of blood became warm fistfuls that released in thuds and gasps. I walked across cold grasses and parted sheaths of field mint and cliff fern, boughs of fir and cedar. And somewhere along the way of all that, I drew breath deep into the socket of my chest, held it for minutes at a time and released it into stars.

At nine years old, Ben's rudimentary bear-aware instincts were spot on. Despite how gangly and awkward and impetuous he approached practically everything else he came across, when we stumbled our way into the company of that live bear, Ben somehow reined his trademark exuberance inward. In doing so, he achieved the feat he seemed to otherwise avoid the whole of his life – he remained still. He stood there, a nine-year old boy in a canary yellow Charlie Brown *Happiness Is a Warm Puppy* sweatshirt with frayed sleeve cuffs, grass stained knees and tangled shoe laces, and he held my tiny form firmly against his chest. He pressed his fingers into my arm to sustain my attention, my compliant motionlessness.

Even though I obeyed, I completely misunderstood the cause inspiring his direction. At five years old, with my brother's arm wrapped around my chest and a round-headed black bear with wet nose and wide eyes aimed at us five feet above our small heads – I was captured in the most amazing and beautiful diorama my short years of life had then provided.

I stood beneath a living, breathing bear – a human-sized mammal resting its weight against thatched oak branches above my head. I watched the bear's eyes move from Ben to me, and back again. I watched the nostrils of his nose flame. I listened to the rasp of his breath.

In the wet cement that comprised my yet developing cerebral cortex, I honestly believed Ben's intent, his hope of that moment, was the same one I felt bloom across my chest. Years later, I realized my brother's actions were instinctively protective. He wanted to keep us from harm. But standing there, beneath the limb-bending young bear who stared into our fixed gazes, I mistook Ben's reach across my chest as a gesture aimed solely at ensuring the scene before us last as long as was earthly possible.

Despite any inaccuracies of interpretation and the ephemeral nature of Ben's mortality, from that moment, and from a thousand others, my brother's firm hands never left my shoulders.

The crisp shoots of the sedge flats are nearly three feet high. They undulate in the wind, and part as though something is forcing its way through. I can see the top of her rounded head. It crests the dewed sea of green. Behind her, the thin blades whisper and sigh.

The first time Clare met both my brothers, Ben and Alex, they had splintered their way through my apartment door. Their two shoulders split the eighty-year-old varnished wood in two solid heaves.

Prior to their break-in, Clare and I heard the muffled voices, mistook them for drunken tenants, and then the tear of wood in the living room, followed by a labored, "Fuuuuuuuuuuuuuuuck..." And then, the tangle of Alex and Ben's groaning laughter.

I leapt from the bed with a sheet wrapped around my waist. Clare threw herself into a robe. "What in the hell?" she said.

Ben was already picking up fragments of the splintered molding and rubbing his shoulder when I dashed into the room.

"Jesus, Ben…" I said. "You can't wait for a guy to answer the door?"

"Normally," answered Ben, his fists full now with door frame shrapnel. "Had no idea the thing was going to open up like that. One heave and it became a set piece from *The Shining*."

Alex appeared more contrite. He stood with his trademark half grin in the shadow of the kitchen doorway. He shook his head.

"It can be – I'm pretty sure it can be glued, though," said Ben.

"Glued?!"

Clare inched her way into the room, her robe belt cinched tight, her hair mussed and cheeks flushed. My brothers' heads turned in unison.

"Oh, shit…" said Ben. "He has a girl, too."

"Told you," mumbled Alex.

"We did knock," said Ben. "Bummer."

"Jesus, Ben," I said, and ran my hand along the open seam in my door. "Really didn't think an oak door like that would – it's oak, right?"

"Pine."

"Really didn't think a pine door – pine, really?"

I handed him a long, fragmented section of the door's former frame. "Hold this."

He clumped the strip of wood with the others, and I leaned forward and socked his shoulder as hard as I could. He dropped the frame pieces and grabbed his arm with a yelp that morphed into contagious laughter.

It was the first I had seen him in six months, this an unannounced stop-over from his semester break in Madison, en route on an impromptu California road trip, my brother Ben, master of surprise entrances and exits and spur of the moment momentum.

"I'm Alex," said my brother. He extended his hand to Clare while running the other one through his mop of hair. "Sorry about all this."

Clare smiled and shook my brother's hand, and then turned to Ben.

"And I'm pretty sure you're Ben," she said.

"We did knock," answered Ben. "Just – Jack doesn't always answer, so we went ahead, you know..." He pulled a half-empty bottle of Jose Cuervo from his overcoat pocket, hoisted it toward us. "I brought this," he said.

His face beamed with the same hopeful anticipation that coupled his every move, the eternal belief that the next moment was worlds more interesting than the one he had already moved past.

When I imagine the world through my brother's eyes in the moment before he lost consciousness, all I see is falling snow. It swims the wide sweep of his headlights — cascading flakes that lift across the plume of his car's projection and over the wet highway that splits the soft hills of western Wisconsin, snow that falls as thick as it did in our childhood, the dense flurries that swept the dark oaks behind our house, cloaked their bark, coated their crossing limbs and branches, and silenced my two brothers and me as we sat behind our dining room sliding glass door and waited to see the avalanche of snow ribbon from the highest limbs in intermittent gusts of wind.

It's what I like to believe – that in his final conscious moments, my brother found himself lost in those same early memories, held in the wonder of the simple beauty of tangled snow, its fall and lift in headlight illumination, the intermittent puckered kisses of flakes against windshield glass, the world stretched before him, one soft, beautiful tableau.

Or maybe the whole world, even its beauty, emptied his mind as his body lurched forward into the pull of gravity. Maybe, in the end, all there is is silence, the moment before impact, a calm that transcends panic, and empties everything but wonder.

When my brother's midnight blue Pontiac swerved against the tail-spray of the semi-tractor trailer outside of Tomah, Wisconsin that late November afternoon – that's how I picture him, locked in awe, his soft lips barely parted.

Ben and his dorm-mate were racing against the light fall of freezing rain and their hopes of making it home to Saint Paul in time for Thanksgiving family dinners. Both of them had just completed the last of their mid-term exams and what would have been their penultimate semester at college. I imagine they were anxious to pass the swaying semi that was likely slowing as a precaution against the icy highway. Maybe they were closer than they should have been when Ben lost control and steered into the moon.

The highway patrol report indicated Ben's Pontiac was traveling near the speed limit when it entered its spin. It noted Ben had held from applying the brakes when he banked into the first skid, adhering to lessons learned through four Minnesota winter driving seasons. The report also noted it was probably the car's close proximity to the semi tailwind that pulled them deeper into the spin, the vacuum of the truck's spent force that sucked them into their wayward pitch, sped their force into the opposing lane, across the pavement and up the bank, where the car sluiced the telephone pole and cleaved it into two neat halves. The windshield burst from the force, popped glass shards severely enough to pock mark the higher limbs of nearby trees.

My family stared at the highway patrol report for hours – each neatly written sentence, each punctuation mark, every measurement and marking. We stared at it as though we believed it would eventually reveal a completely different outcome than it did.

Ben's roommate died on impact, his body in pieces along the asphalt and in the belly of the ditch. His family would never again see his body whole. Ben never regained consciousness. He remained alive, his face blue and sliced from chin to ear, his nose pushed sideways into his skull. He remained alive for the duration it took the rescue crew to saw his shoeless, limp body free from the compressed cab frame and rush him to Tomah Fairview, the clouds through the ambulance windshield as purple as the bruise across his chest – the deformed shape of the steering wheel column that had split his rib cage. He remained alive through two consecutive surgeries and the seventeen weeks we circled his hospital bed and waited for him to emerge from the tangle of I.V. lines and heart monitor wires that banked his hospital bed. His body was swollen nearly twice its normal size.

The miraculous thing about losing someone you love, a family member, is how the world around you moves right past you in its continued whir. You find yourself suspended in awe. Nothing is different. Nothing is changed. But your body floats in an imagined ocean.

That's when it started. Not long after my brother's life slipped past us, the first bear approached. It crept through my dreams the night after my brother died, nimbly enough I barely noticed it. It swaggered through the open door frame. It leaned against the mattress. The moist cowl of its breath warmed the side of my face.

I follow her to the edge of the silt pond, watch her broad snout nudge the flowered water lilies. Her two rounded ears silhouette against moon.

The last time I saw Ben conscious, he sat across the table from me in a Marlboro T-shirt and mirrored Ray-Bans. The three of us were huddled around a small table: Ben, Alex and me, in a smoke filled bar in Uptown, Minneapolis. The bass line from a muddy sounding jukebox vibrated the legs of our chairs. The bar was dark enough to warrant the use of night vision goggles to view your glass of beer in front of you, but Ben continued wearing his sunglasses regardless, the wide grin beneath them the only part of him visible from the short distance. It was the night before he would be leaving for his senior year at Madison, and we were drinking Coors and debating which of the three of us had put our parents through the worst of it.

"What's to compare?" said Ben. "Combined, you two don't even come close."

"Two weeks before I left for college," countered Alex, "I hadn't talked to Dad for, like, the last three weeks. I went through this adjustment period or something. I couldn't talk to anyone, especially him, and he finally asked me to take a walk with him, you know, to figure out why. And half way through the walk, I told him I didn't want my life to mirror his. That was the problem. I didn't want to be him."

"Jesus," I said.

"Maybe he focused on the fact you took the time to compare your life with his," said Ben.

"Knowing Dad," said Alex, "he was probably just relieved I was at least talking to him again."

"You guys have any idea how long my rap sheet is?" asked Ben.

"Here it comes," I said.

"Mom and Dad were in the god-damned principal's office so many times, people mistook them for staff. Half the social studies wing – no, I mean it, had signed a petition to have my ass expelled. I lodged Dad's Jeep into the marsh. And only after I stole the keys and disconnected the odometer."

"As if anyone would have noticed the mileage," said Alex.

"Or cared," I added.

"You school yourself on *Mission Impossible* episodes," said Ben, "results follow. And I had no idea that god damned marsh was so…"

"What?" said Alex. "Wet?"

"I got caught," continued Ben, "how many times with nickel bags in my jean jacket, ripped the door off their bedroom that time."

"Don't forget that party you threw when they left town," I said, "when you nearly burned the house down."

"Cigarette butts and bottle caps are still spitting out the kitchen sink when it backs up," said Alex.

"Exactly," said Ben. "Can either of you name one time you fucked up something so bad carpet had to be replaced? The whole damned living room? Name one."

"I wonder what was worse," I said. "The number of fiascos you committed or the ineptness you repeatedly applied covering your tracks."

Ben's grin erupted into his staccato laugh, louder than the bar's jukebox.

"Seriously, Ben. Decide to rob a china shop, you'd ride in through the doors on a blind camel."

"A blind camel with Tourette's," said Alex.

Ben's laughter climbed. His head fell back in a cackle. Nearby bar patrons turned to the table with the three men erupting until tears ran their faces.

When she pulls herself to the muddy bank, moonlight paints her wide shoulders. She lowers her head, and the darkness swallows her form.

Clare stayed with me in my tiny Minneapolis apartment the first six weeks following Ben's death. She took an hour or two at a time to run to the university to pick up texts, attend a class, or stop in at her dorm. She was a little more than a year away from completing her undergraduate degree, something I had shelved – I dropped all my classes mid-semester after Ben's accident.

I was living, then, in a basement apartment near campus, tangled octopus arms of hot water piping knitted across the ceiling.

After Ben's funeral, after the tumult of helping my family plan it and then the divide and conquer mission of fielding the seemingly unending stream of condolences and awkward gestures of sympathy, I retreated to the apartment like a bear to a den. And then, with little to occupy my time, I remained as still as I could, hours at a time. I minimized the expanse of my chest, each breath. If I could slow my heart, that single muscle, maybe I could bay the sea of pain circling it.

Clare assumed the duo role of nursemaid and girlfriend, and at twenty years old, balanced the competing responsibilities of student and individual savior. Ours was suddenly a vastly different relationship from the one we were buoyantly exploring prior to Ben's death.

She hurried home during her break between classes with a demi loaf of milk bread, still warm, from the French bakery down the block. She spread a towel across my living room floor and set large bowls of Mrs. Grass boxed chicken noodle soup, swirling steam. We dunked torn pieces of bread into the soup and devoured them. Our chins dripped broth.

Single-handedly, she sustained me through this new storm, if only through the warm and salty comfort of Mrs. Grass chicken broth and noodles and her own reliable company.

When she hurried off to class again, I resumed my motionless trance. I practiced bear breaths. I stared out windows. And every time the silence was interrupted by the sound of turned security latch of the apartment building door, my heart lifted. Like a wounded animal yearning warmth, comfort, I listened for Clare's soft footsteps descending the stairs.

One night, I wandered from bed into the dark living room. I sat still for nearly an hour, and then Clare noticed my absence in the bed and stepped quietly toward me. Blue light swam through the picture window, across our skin, and my body lurched forward in restrained sobs. Clare knelt beside me. She ran her hand along my curved spine in wide, slow strokes.

"Come back to bed," she whispered. "This will get better. But you really need sleep. We both do."

I watched a single tear dot her knee and roll slowly over its soft curve.

There was what felt like a whole sea within me, a burgeoning squall gathering force, an ever-widening storm, transforming, cell-by-cell, the person I had been. I was watching it happen with the same mute and transfixed gaze Clare was.

The only world I had known, the spinning, humid sphere that contained my two brothers, no longer existed. It had vanished. I was clueless how to respond. And I felt as though I was waiting for Clare — someone, to tell me to let the sadness empty into whatever shape it fell into. Without that encouragement, I continued to rein in, contain and dampen, afraid of all that would spill out if I let it, frightened of what world might replace the former one I knew, afraid to find out who, if anyone, might be left standing in the center of it, along with me.

I sat on the floor, and Clare stroked my back. She took my elbow and led me back into the bedroom, sat me on the bed. I lifted her cotton camisole over her head. She raised her arms, her eyes locked into mine. Her long, brown hair fell across her face and shoulder. I pressed my face into her neck, rested my hand against the oval birthmark on her waist. I pulled her close. I felt her warmth, the blood pulse along her neck.

"Don't please let go," I asked her. "Wherever this leads, don't let go."

She lifted my head in the cup of her small palm, her eyes into mine. "There will never be that," she said so quietly, I could barely hear, and she pulled me toward her, her heart a rapid metronome against my chest.

I follow a pair of them. They amble down the avalanche-washed debris. They step over the veins of melt that seep through grit and rock. Intermittently, they lift their heads and sniff and then circle the outwash and rake their claws into mud. They tear open the thawing soil and pull stone and ice with their forepaws, oblivious to its ringing trail down the slope.

While Clare was occupied at campus, I found a new study of mine own — self-directed. It required motionlessness, heavy blankets pulled around me, a barricade of cover-worn biology texts surrounding my body in the shape of an expanding fan.

I consumed my time, my imagination, my continual thoughts with the dreams of bears – soft clouds of gnats hovering over ponds, supple, green grasses trembling in southern breezes, blanket flowers and wild crocus — whatever terrestrial images I could think of that might linger in their memory as they drifted across the river of torpor.

It was simply that – their winter sleep, their hibernation I was most interested in. I wanted to understand how their hearts transitioned from the hammer of fifty to ninety contractions per minute into eight – ambient life flow sustained by low waves drifting farther and farther across a wide sea. I wanted to find my way to the same mute place in the universe, the same aqueous tether.

I see them through the blue cedar, across the swale of clover. They move, one by one, across the alpine meadow. I count six bears, each with its head bowed. They move through the giant shadows of trees. The one in the lead stands on its haunches, elbows extended. Its forepaws are bent toward the earth.

Our first date, mine and Clare's, three years before Ben's death, evolved into a twelve-hour road trip into western Wisconsin. We stopped to capture images with a drugstore disposable camera: Clare feigning panic at a lion-headed fountain, her small head locked between its gaping jaws; me posed in a pasture of curious cows. We bought wax paper-wrapped grilled cheese sandwiches from a small diner and consumed them in my car with the heater running. The car windows clouded from our breath and the moist heat of gooey cheese sandwiches and piping cups of cider clasped in our hands.

Falling in love with her was as easy as breathing.

It was early April the first time I met her parents. My heart lurched when I walked across the open patches of snow on their front lawn to ring the doorbell. During dinner, Clare's jowl-faced basset hound vacuumed an untended chicken wing from my absently guarded plate and snorted it whole before I could muster protest, and I sweat out the remainder of the evening covertly checking the dog's abdomen for any signs of chicken wing bones protruding through muscle.

The friendly basset hound, thankfully, had a hardy digestive track; no casualties, canine or human.

I don't think either one of us, me or Clare, was prepared to fall as deeply or merge our lives as quickly as we did. The connection, the ease of it, seemed to catch us both by surprise. One month, we were introducing ourselves, dipping our toes in the water of mutual attraction, and the next we were contentedly joined, listing against each other's soft body. I remember the late June rain that pushed us through a field of foxglove and clover and how the earth smelled like broken flowers. We wove our way to a shelter of cottonwood and held each other. We laughed through the shivering, until the rain subsided and all that was left was wind through the cold leaves and my hands against Clare's naked waist, her skin warm and wet, my mouth against her neck, her hair like wet ivy across her lips. We told each other nothing else would ever matter as much, as much as this.

And between us and surrounding us, nothing did.

We held each other through entire nights, watched the sky through the windows warm from blue to amber, the stars, one after the last, disappear. Our warm bodies, our wet mouths leaned into one another's as if searching for a hidden seam, an invisible universe.

We drew breath in time, lost completely in the other, just there, just breathing, the two of us simply leaning all the way into whatever opening emerged.

They move against the current, and their massive bodies split the moon's reflection into scattered stars and slivers. Their humped shoulders push river eddies to the shoreline. From my view above them, they look like whales in a darkened ocean, broad backed orca. In the wider pools, they lunge and disappear. Their dives push thick waves toward shore.

When ten whole months had elapsed past Ben's death, I had perfected the art of slowing my pulse, moments at a time, to half its normal rate – only twice the meter of a denned bear's – a moderate triumph I kept secret.

My bedroom had become little more than a wrinkled berth of covers and firmly indented pillows. A sprawl of bear books and articles surrounded my mattress.

It was September. Clare was back at school. She had attempted, in vain, to get me to resume my education and join her.

"I don't want to start a whole new semester by myself," she told me. "And I don't think it's good for you to remain locked in whatever place this is you're in."

I didn't know how to tell her I had reasonable certainty I could – remain locked there. Contentedly immobile.

My savings depleted, I left notice at my apartment and winterized a cube-shaped storage unit my father originally framed years before on the lake property we owned an hour north of Saint Paul: a hamlet of marshland brimming with duckweed and cattails that elevated to an isthmus of land perched above a comma-shaped lake.

Aside from my winter bear heart rate experiment, it was the first time I put effort into anything since Ben's death, transforming a partially constructed storage unit into a place I could live a while. I didn't have any plans beyond that.

The simple plywood structure was ten feet square, a solid enclosure over wood joists and concrete footings. The interior was exposed studs, rain-stained plywood flooring, and swallow nests mudded into the upper corners.

I moved stored lawn mowers, bicycles and boxes of musty books into a rented storage unit. I swept the floor of swallow droppings and sawed a seven-foot wide square through one wall. Sawdust ticked my face as I moved the circular saw through the wood, and opened the view to the lake; I framed and installed a sliding glass door in its place. With my father's help, I moved an old iron wood stove into the far corner, cut a hole through the roof and stacked metal flue sections all the way into the trees. With 2-by-6 framing, we nailed a loft platform along one half of the room where I unfurled my sleeping bag. Above it, I cut a circular hole in the wall and dropped a round window in place. At night, moonlight pooled across my forehead.

By mid October, the cracks between plywood had all been sealed with silicone, the studs insulated with fiberglass batts and protected from moisture by a stapled sheet of 4mil poly, finished with tongue and groove pine carsiding nailed over it. I chain sawed dead trees and split the wood, banked a massive woodpile near the marsh. I sat by the lake and stared out at the water and the leaf thinning trees surrounding it.

"How long do you plan on staying here?" Clare asked, her cheeks red from the autumn chill.

"Through the winter, I guess," I said.

"And no more?" She paced the floor of my newly appointed home. She eyed the details of construction – the wood stove, the lofted bed platform, the tongue and groove pine siding.

"Can we think about looking for an apartment together this spring, then?" she asked. "I was thinking it was time for that."

"Maybe," I answered. "I just need to do this, first."

"What will you do here?"

"I'm really not sure I'm going to do much of anything."

Clare didn't push. She continued her coursework, her life separate from mine Monday through Friday. On weekends, she drove out and joined me. She buried herself in her texts and notebooks, nursed cups of whiskey and tea with me at night, her legs covered in blankets. We listened to music and stared into the starred sky.

We also made love with a silent ferocity we hadn't before known, as though the one place holding us together lay between our two naked bodies. The ending often found one or both of us with our face wet in emotion.

Clare slept beside me, and I slipped out of her arms, quietly lowered myself from the loft platform. The wood stove hissed and popped freshly split birch. I wandered along the shore in starlight. The tufted and weathered cattails nodded in the wind, and the moon was milky and low. I listened to the breezes through the tendrils of willow – whispers and sighs.

There were nights like this, many in a row, where I couldn't force myself to sleep.

I wanted to wake Clare. I wanted to breathe into the curve of her neck, open my fingers across her chest, kiss her awake, and take her by the hand to my places along the lake. I wanted to tell her how much I missed Ben, how I didn't know my way in the world without his place in it too, and how indelibly I missed her, also. I wanted her to know how far away I felt from everything.

Sometimes, I rested whole nights by the lake, and stared across its dark surface from the hammock stretched between oaks; their limbs moaned in the wind. My body was cold and stiff when I returned to find Clare brushing her hair in the reflection of the sliding glass door, her expression sad.

"Think about coming into the city this week," she said. "Even for one evening. We'll see a show, have dinner out, something simple and new."

By early November, the marsh froze overnight, a thin skin of ice that melted during sunny days and froze again. One month more, snow fell whole days at a time.

When I missed Clare, I drove to the Standard station and called her from the pay phone just to hear her voice. I pressed my ear as close against the cold phone as I could, and I pretended I could feel her warm breath. The nights I called, and she didn't answer, found me heartbroken, lost. The nights she did answer, I found little to say.

January arrived in a series of some of the coldest successive nights we'd known in years, nights so cold, I swore I could hear the stars split into two, nights I sat close to the wood stove, my hands inches from its surface, palms open. Sometimes I left the cabin for hours to cross country ski across the lake in the ruts of snowmobile tracks welded into snow. My lungs ached from the frigid air. Other times I merely watched the stars through my round window. Or I hunkered next to a small, portable battery operated black and white television set tuned to a wash of gray static, its sonorous white noise a suitable backdrop to the low-grade trance I remained locked in.

The worst part was remembering how completely in love I was before my brother's car skidded across that distant asphalt. I tried not to, because every time I did the contrast between then and now hurt. How couldn't it? But her soft face, Clare's sweet face, lifted to the surface – through knotted, low winter clouds: Clare's green, flecked eyes; in the hiss of flame: Clare's red lips. I missed her in pieces; I missed her everywhere.

Strange how our singular, though significant, losses can turn the rest of our lives in invisible, unforeseeable knots. Or how our lives that came before can seem to hover mid-air, where we hope they'll remain until we can safely retrieve them.

I spent one whole week remembering the soft curve of Clare's knee, the tiny freckles like birds in sky along the oval dent of her kneecap, the smooth skin and miniscule nest of blue veins on the back, above the calf muscle. I sketched drawings of her knee in pencil, tacked them to the wall. When she showed up at the lake the following weekend, I begged her to undress so I could photograph both knees, both calves, and I didn't relent until she did.

"You need a photograph of my knees? Knees? Really?"

"I miss every part of you when you're not next to me," I told her.

"My knees?" she said, her back against the floor, knees balled into her chest. She pulled free her blue jeans.

"Especially your knees. Your knees. The cusp between your lips. The small of your back. The backward spiral of the lightest hair on the back of your neck. Every part."

Sometimes at night, without her near, I fell so intensely into the warm memory of early courtship: the runs we made across fields – kites lofting toward clouds; their string wrapped around our fingers, Clare sitting on my lap, her hands gently cupping each side of my face, our naked bodies pressed against each other. *"This is as close as two bodies can merge into each other, isn't it?"* she asked. *"In a single breath, have you ever been more happy or more sad?"* and she pressed closer and closer against me, her mouth against mine.

Never more happy. Never more sad.

By the end of March, photographs – black and white fragmented images of Clare, Clare's knees, her calves, her shoulders, fingers, lips, ears, eyes, breasts, the balls of her feet, toes – the deconstruction and reconstruction of her via 5x7 black and white grainy images – hung across my wall, anchored by push pins around the perimeter of my cube-shaped winter shelter.

I was willing myself to hurt past the point of hurting. I believed I could separate myself from everything that mattered to me, everyone I loved, and miss them all at once and then return renewed, cleansed, as though there was a center of grief I could finally swallow and then move my life past. But no matter how far into it I bit, there were always miles left to chew.

They lumber through the talus and the boulder-strewn field, and they sniff for the larger clusters of moths. They stand short distances from one another and excavate newly located hordes and lunge into the cool soil. They devour moths en masse, and snap at those that lift into sky.

The gravel field sways with moth-feeding bears.

At night, the snow across the lake looked mineral blue. Our gait was halted by all the rutted snowmobile tracks we trudged across, the serrated chunks of splayed ice and snow, and I led Clare to the ice fishing house I had discovered west of the point. Unlike the other icehouses moored across the lake, this one's plywood hinged door was sans padlock, making it an obvious mid-lake shelter for trespassers like me.

Beneath our feet, the frozen lake rumbled a muffled thunder, booms and long snapping cracks of the massive sheet of ice straining over the hidden water mass. We could feel the vibration beneath our feet at each new pop and groan.

"You get used to those sounds," I told Clare.

I could barely see Clare's eyes peering at me above her wool scarf, wrapped thrice around her head; her breath fogged through it. The winds were light but it was minus eight degrees.

"As long as it's safe to walk across," she said. Her mittened hands were tucked beneath her parka armpits.

"It's safe," I told her. "Cars drive across it. At this point, you'd need a meteor to break it open."

"Good," said Clare. Her clipped steps gathered speed behind me.

Another long boom echoed beneath our feet. I felt its tremor in my knees.

"I love that, though," I told her. "I like to pretend I'm walking across a thawing serpent's spine. And those groans are its empty stomach."

"You do that, then," said Clare. "But maybe to yourself."

I opened the door, and Clare entered. She stepped across the ice floor and its frozen auger scars, and sat on the wooden bench along the wall, her knees together, mittened hands between them.

"So, show me this secret trick of yours," she said, seemingly anxious. When I lit a candle, she unwrapped her scarf. She waited for her sight to adjust to the candlelit walls.

"I can't promise this is going to work," I told her. I leaned against the far wall of the icehouse and slid to the iced floor. "It takes concentration. A lot. And I've only done this on my own; never an audience."

"What do I need to do?"

"I don't know – just, I mean, try to be still," I told her. "Place your fingers across the side of my neck to feel my pulse. Count the seconds between."

"For how long?" she asked.

"Until the seconds between them stretch to eight or nine or ten."

"Between pulses?"

"Pulses."

"Of your heart," she said, her voice lower.

Clare stared at me from the icehouse bench. She breathed a thin sigh of frosted air, and her mouth birthed a smile.

"If I get there," I said. "And it may take a good five or ten minutes. It's possible I may drift off a bit."

"Okay," she said. "No way are you being serious."

"Look," I said. "It may not even work. Go with me on this. If you can."

"Wait. This is the secret thing you wanted to show me?" she asked. "I don't really get it."

I shifted my concentration from Clare's clouded breath and the light press of her fingers beneath my jaw to the moaning heave of the frozen lake beneath me. Each new rumble became the groan of bears, and I lost count of the time passing, and then Clare repeated my name and pressed her hands so deep into my shoulders, it hurt. Her face was close enough to mine, I could feel her warm breath. Her eyes were whole moons.

"What in the hell?" she muttered. She lifted her fingers from my neck.

I stared into her wet eyes, her open mouth. My lungs filled with breath.

"Jack," she said. "I mean, what is all this?"

"How long did it take?" I asked.

"I don't know, she said. "Maybe four minutes. Four minutes, and your pulse slowed to a whisper. I could barely feel it."

"How many seconds between them?"

"Ten seconds," she said, so quietly I could barely hear.

"Don't you think – come on, isn't that pretty amazing?"

Clare was silent.

"I mean, seriously – did you even think it was possible?"

She stared at me, expressionless.

"Six to eight beats a minute," I said. "That's a bear's heart rate in the middle of hibernation."

"And you're – I mean, that's what you're trying to replicate? Why?"

I don't know what I was looking for from Clare. After four months of living in stoic silence in a cube shaped shelter next to a nearly abandoned lake, I had asked her to follow me across its ice and made her count the beats of my heart until they waned into single thuds across whole minutes. It was as if I was conspiring to have her join me in some ursine-inspired Capulet and Montague hemlock sleep over. As though I envisioned us happily supine, our fingers woven, eyes closed to the stars above our heads, our arteries chanting the faintest murmurs of life beneath our skin. My vision of *happily ever after* was becoming distorted beyond even my own recognition.

"It's an experiment," I told her. "Meditation."

Clare was quiet.

"It feels different than that," she said. "It doesn't feel, I don't know, that healthy. Or even healing. It feels like a going away. Sometimes I feel like you're trying to burrow yourself so far into the loss of Ben, you're leaving barely any of yourself for me, for anyone, to grab hold of. At some point, I have to wonder, how much of it is on purpose?"

I thought of what Clare was suggesting, and wished I had an explanation that would relieve her of fear, a tangible motive that would transition her bewilderment to support, but nothing leaped immediately to mind.

On our wordless trek back to the cabin, I regretted dragging Clare all the way across the ice to show her something she wasn't ready for, something I couldn't adeptly explain. I had surmised sharing my secret accomplishment would somehow bring us closer, as though Clare would immediately volunteer for the role of magician's assistant, no questions asked. Instead, I only hoped she'd soon forget the event entirely. Maybe we could go back to being okay again if she would just forget this one episode, and if I could keep the rest of it, my grand experiment, all to myself.

I move farther into the wood, closer to them, into the moss and sedges. I can hear their steps through the soapberry bushes, the snap of twigs. I move close enough I can hear their breathing – long, deep sighs. I reach my arm through the leaves and feel their warm breath against my skin.

When the lake finally opened to thaw, the shifting sheet of ice had dozed rolls of sand and soil along the shoreline. It was April. I spent early mornings walking the perimeter on the last solid shelf of the winter freeze. Lake water oozed up through the wayward fractures I walked across. I was sorry to see it go, the thawing lake ice moving to the center in sheets of slush, an old friend disappearing.

Soon, the house finches swarmed the feeder. Then the Grosbeaks, then warblers. Sunflower husks and spent millet mounded across the newly thawed timothy. For a while, I kept a tally of each new bird I spotted. The house finches remained in a solid lead; their mottled red bodies clustered into masses of fidgeting feathers and beaks. And sometimes the grackles would descend into the trees a hundred at a time and momentarily fill the woods with staccato chatter before they lifted in a curtain of oily black feathers and wings.

We had a long stretch of rains that spring, day-long soaks that gnawed the remaining ice and snow and wore it away. Cumulonimbus, with saturated umber, anchored the horizon and burst downpours of hail and cold rain and wind that bent the trunks of trees and split willow wide open. In the tail of each storm, I sat the edge of the shoreline and listened to the wet, dripping trees.

You could smell the nearby pastures as the sun warmed them, newly tilled soil and manure – their sweet musk.

I wanted to tell my family about the bears. I wanted to tell them how they collected in my dreams ever since Ben's death, how they arrived, solo or in clusters of two or three, and how sometimes, they gathered in swaying fields until their collected shapes blotted the horizon. I wanted to tell my mother, my father, and my brother Alex how I could sometimes feel the bears' breath against my face; how it smelled of salmon blood and fermented roots and moth wings; and how I yearned to stretch my fingers into their matted chests and pull my face deep into its thatch. How the dreamt bears were becoming the only thing I believed in: my new extended family, the warm wall enveloping me.

When lightning storms bloomed, I hid in the lee of the oak with my father's Nikon camera strapped around my neck and attempted to capture flashes of lightning on film, the bright fireball flashes between dark limbs. It veined through clouds. On clear nights, I watched the moon ford across sky. I sat and wondered how I should let Clare know I had decided to move to Montana, to follow bears into the woods. I wondered how to ask her to join me there, what her answer would be about moving 1100 miles from the only home we knew. Because of bears.

Close up, the matted fur across his broad chest is blue and black. The shadow of his huge form cloaks me. His breath is river moss and sky. He locks his forelegs across my shoulder blades. His claws cleave my shirt and skin. His barrel-shaped torso thrusts against my chin. I close my eyes and feel protected. I burrow my face deeper into his warm chest, my ear pressed against his thundering heart.

Missoula, Montana

A T FOUR A.M., MISSOULA, MONTANA is pockets of light reflected across a dark river – convenience store gas stations and isthmuses of houses muscled into a wide swale of curving mountain. I drove straight through, only stopping my pick-up truck and the swaying U-Haul locked in place behind my rear bumper after winding up Pattee Canyon Drive, a road that curves across the face of Mount Sentinel to a plateau that overlooks the spill of lights and the twist of the mill smoke, telephone crosses, blue in the moon, sutured by wire. I turned the key from the ignition, and then got out of the truck, walked five paces across the asphalt to a split rail fence, inhaled, peed, and stared at the incandescent lights of Missoula below me.

What in the hell am I doing here? Twenty-six hours of freeway from Minnesota, I trembled in wonder.

I contemplated turning tail, right then and there, before witnessing the first trace of morning sunlight. But then, I heard the cows approaching me, scattered bovines chewing brittle stems of grass, swaying shapes in the darkness. It was company enough to calm my nerves – a field of silent cows.

I walked to my pick-up truck and pulled my twin mattress from the back, hoisted it over the fence, dragged it sideways across the field, and dropped it. I unlocked the door latch of the U-Haul, retrieved my sleeping bag and the pillow nestled between the boxes. I grabbed my battery operated portable black and white television. Again, I cleared the fence, wandered into the field and set each of the items on the mattress.

I crawled into my sleeping bag, set the television on my chest and clicked it on. Phosphorous hiss and static shifted across the field, flickered through the fence line, and reflected the telephone pole glass insulators.

I cinched the bag around my face. I was fully entombed, bedded on a single mattress in the elevated Montana pasture. The black and white television whispered static across my chest. My eyes were saucers. I stared up into the clouds. My whole body was bathed in the blue wash of a portable television, my cathode ray cocoon.

I thought of Clare and her sweet face, and wished her next to me, her warm breath, and I thought of a thousand reasons she should be, and ten thousand more she shouldn't.

The blue, hissing television swam static into the clouds.

The television's hum vibrated the bones of my chest through the night. I opened my eyes to the dawning sun, and my mattress was surrounded by grazing cows. One followed me when I untangled myself from my sleeping bag and wandered over the ridge where I crouched between two scraggly bushes and shat. The trailing cow stared at me through the full act. And then I heard a gate latch fall and a cattle gate swing open. I hoisted my pants and turned. My cow companion loped toward the sound.

When I cleared the ridge, a man in blue jeans and gray plaid shirt was standing next to my mattress. A shotgun rested in the crook of his arm.

"Fuck is this?" he grumbled.

"Whoa," I said. "Hey!"

"Is this a fucking television set?" he asked, and nudged it with the barrel of his shotgun.

"I'm trespassing, I suppose."

"You suppose?"

"It was late when I got here. Seriously, it was hard to see where I was."

"Is this a fucking TV?"

"Let me get that back in my truck."

His expression merged the emotions of disbelief and annoyance.

"You slept here last night?" he asked.

His eyes darted from cow to cow, taking inventory, as if I had butchered one of them and slung its hind end over a campfire spit for dinner.

"I just got into town. I was tired. I mean yes, I guess I did sleep here, but – "

"You *guess*? You haul your mattress onto my land and help yourself to forty winks? Like this was a god damned hotel room or something? You see any bibles wedged next to the cattle trough?"

It was a random enough question, you had to wonder about the follow-up.

"I'm guessing you can't camp on property here without permission," I said.

The man paused and glared at me.

"Can you *any*where?" he asked.

"Sweden," I said, and the man's face seemed to knot like clouds.

"Who the hell are you?"

"I'm just – "

"Sweden? Are you fucking with me?"

"Just answering your question."

"Buddy, if you think this is Sweden, you better go wipe the lutefisk off your roadmap and take another look."

That's when I made error in reading his remark as humor, a gesture to alleviate the tension.

"You do bear a resemblance to Max von Sydow," I said and smiled.

"Get off my *fucking property!*" He bellowed loud enough, the cows uniformly paused their chewing. And then he leaned forward, and the barrel of his shotgun discharged and blew a shell through the center of my mattress. In retrospect, I don't think he meant to fire. If he had, he probably wouldn't have jumped nearly the height I did in response. But at the moment, my sole reality was the haze of sulfur and polyester mattress fiber that swam the air.

I yelped and lowered my head. My hands reached into the sky, and I stared at the charred hole ripped through the mattress ticking and the rabid tufts of foam protruding from its mouth.

When I looked back up, the man's face resembled a sugar beet, freshly unearthed from soil. "You happy now?" he asked.

Full disclosure, I couldn't be more unhappy. Or more panicked. Knowing next to nothing about firearms, I had to assume these things were capable of housing more than one shell at a time. And that a man drawn to the avocation of mattress target practice, on purpose or by accident, was capable of worse.

"Look," I said. "What works for you here? In this situation?" I tempered my voice with the calmest conversational tone I could muster, figured it the shortest distance toward de-escalation.

"Works for me?"

"To erase this entire scene from your day?" I said. "From both our days?"

He stared at me a duration that probably consumed all of five seconds but seemed, given the circumstances, multiplied by dog years.

"You can start by getting your shit off my property," he said.

I assumed he meant my referential shit, as in gut shot mattress, sleeping bag and portable television, not my actual shit, of which he wasn't yet aware or would have commenced blasting the hell out of that, too, or of the portion of my body from whence it came.

"Got it," I said. "All shit, off your property."

"I'm getting back in my outfit," he said. "I'm driving into town. And when I get back, there won't be a single sign of your bunny hugger ass ever having been here."

"Jesus!" I said. "You just blasted a hole through the center of my mattress. Large enough to lob softballs through! You really think I want to hang around and read the paper?! I want out of here as badly as you want me to be."

He broke the shotgun from the crook of his arm and marched back through the fence gate and grumbled a statement, barely audible except for the words "Norwegian degenerate." Then he hoisted himself back into his idling pick-up truck and slowly pulled away, staring back at me the whole while.

When his truck disappeared, I stared at the warm hole torn through my mattress, charred cilia.

I paced to the fence line and stared at the valley. My heart clunked around my rib cage like a squirrel trapped in a furnace. And then I made a move known in football terms as "taking a knee," but it was a whole lot less graceful than the manual suggests. The soil was cold, wet. It bled through my jeans.

"Pretty sure that could have gone better," I said aloud, to no one.

The sun glinted off the western-facing windows of the houses of Missoula below. To my right, a large, white monogrammed "M" was embedded in Mount Sentinel, marking the university campus for each airplane passenger landing at Johnson Bell County Airport and each car banking this stretch of I-90. A hawk drifted by. Its shadow clipped the hillside. I followed its glide all along the distant bend of the Clark Fork River, over the rambled clutch of buildings that comprise this small, western city.

I walked back to my mattress, stuck my hand into its gaping hole. The charred ticking was still warm. I pulled it over my shoulder, a wounded soldier from the trenches, and slipped it into my pick-up bed. My fingers still trembled.

I drove into downtown Missoula and found a newspaper and coffee. I circled a half dozen ads in the rental listings, and dialed their numbers from the Sinclair pay phone.

Weighing the risks of sleeping, uninvited, on someone's real estate a second night, I rented the first apartment I visited, a gold-carpeted one bedroom, with molding and woodwork the color of tea. An imitation glass chandelier hung in the dining area from a gold chain looped across the living room. The room smelled of Lysol and fried trout. I signed the lease, walked to Albertsons and bought an arm load of tomato soup cans, a package of sliced Swiss cheese, and returned to my new apartment, and my mattress. I waited four whole days before emerging again to unload the U-Haul a box at a time.

My neighbors across the alley got out of their blue Chevy Impala in square dancing outfits, and I picked up the phone and dialed Clare's number. The man sported a silky black western shirt and the woman was in a prairie skirt and petticoat. My index finger hovered over the phone keypad as I watched them.

When Clare answered my calls anymore, there was immediate relief followed by the soft bloom of sadness over the distance between us.

"Turns out none of the homesickness gets much better," I told her.

"You just got there," said Clare. "Give it some time."

"I've got neighbors getting out of their car in square dancing outfits. Another I caught lassoing a chair in the backyard with a rope."

"It can't be solely that."

"I swear to god, Clare. This guy was my age, and he was practicing rodeo roping skills out in his yard with a bar stool."

"Oh, lord…"

"If you come across a rogue set of Stickley chairs in the prairie, I know a guy that can rustle the rascals."

Clare laughed.

"Mostly I totter around though town like a clown in a silent movie. Seriously. I feel like an astronaut fucking around on the moon."

"Give it some time," she said. "Wait for the adjustment to, you know, take hold."

Clare reminded me it would only be until Christmas, the first of the year at the latest when she could come join me. She had already been accepted into the University of Montana geography graduate program, was merely tying up the loose ends of her undergraduate degree while I got our place settled for us in Montana. And even though I wondered how ready I was to be a full-time boyfriend again, I mostly just missed and wanted her near. Alone in Montana, I felt perilously adrift.

"Yes, just Christmas until then," I said.

"Have you met with this Krystoff, yet?" she asked, equating, I wondered, a bear researcher with a psychologist, hoping my interaction with a professional expert, wildlife if not behavioral, would lead to some resolve for me. "Have you made sure he has a place for you, you know, in the study?"

"Met with, no."

"But you have made contact, right?"

"Jesus, Clare. You act as though I drove all the way out here without figuring any of this out."

"You have been there nearly two weeks."

"And getting settled first," I said. "Let me tell you, it's no picnic finding your way in a completely new city."

"Even a small one surrounded by woods?"

"Even a small one, surrounded – the setting's not the issue. It's more to do with…remembering how to take part in something again. I've been out of it. Out – of everything."

"I know. I'm sorry."

Jeff Krystoff was a biology professor at the University of Montana and a celebrated bear researcher heading up a first of its kind non-invasive grizzly tracking initiative in the Scapegoat Wilderness of western Montana. After reading about the study, I had contacted him to ask if I could join his volunteer army with the potentially misguided goal of following bears into woods. But now that I arrived, even I had started to question the logic of the choice.

"I didn't mean to be pushy," said Clare. "You know what you're doing. And, anyway, it's a huge shift in your world, your life. I get that."

"My neighbors are square dancers and chair ropers," I reminded her. "My first night here, some jackass shot a hole into the center of my mattress."

"And of course there's that," she said, and snorted a laugh.

"Anyway," I told her. "The woods surrounding this city are beautiful. I wish you and I were in them. Together in them."

I spent the first three weeks of that August avoiding the phone, delaying contact with Krystoff. Instead, I emerged from my dreary apartment inches at a time, like a lost cat from the neighbor's cellar.

I started with the campus grounds. I paced the perimeter of the oval-shaped promenade, anchored in the center by the large, cast bronze grizzly bear statue – that part I liked. I poked my nose down the streets of downtown, down Alder Street and the line of dusty pawn shop windows, the various bars in separate corners of downtown: Charlie B's, The Oxford, The Missoula Club, Red's, The Raven, The Top Hat.

I made my way into the more remote reaches, the winding trail of

Rattlesnake Creek Park where I could walk the shale banked trail and listen to my footsteps through leaves and over earth.

I took long drives through the wide spread of the Bitterroots, roads that shouldered clear-cut mountain slopes and emptied into long stretching valleys. I found forested alcoves where I parked my truck and took lengthy hikes through Lodgepole pine, paper birch and spruce, snowberry and spirea, western red cedar and hemlock. I walked windblown meadows of beargrass. My life was as quiet and unstructured as the one I had left behind.

One night, I wandered the wide football field behind Mount Sentinel High School, a block from my apartment. The close cut, dewed lawn was cold beneath my bare feet. I spotted a line of blocking dummies stored alongside the running track. In the moonlight, they appeared as sentries on watch, their padded torsos – heads and shoulders spaced uniformly, in fives and twos, bolted to metal sleds.

"Evening, gentlemen," I said.

I watched them a moment and then paced twenty yards back and turned. I dipped my finger into my mouth and then into air, tested wind direction for the imaginary kick return. The line of dummies was far enough into the distance, I could barely decipher their moonlit forms.

I crouched and then sprinted. My eyes closed, I ran with all the might I could muster. I aimed my run toward the center dummy but missed my target a finger's width. The dummy's hard shoulder spiked the center of my chest.

I fell to the earth with a groan and sharp, piercing pain that flooded with each following gulp of breath. I felt sick, waited patiently for the nausea to pass. When it didn't, I turned and threw up. That made it hurt more.

I pressed my fingers lightly against three ribs I could tell within reasonable certainty were fractured and against several more that weren't. For a while, I concentrated on taking steadier, shallower breaths. Mount Sentinel's low shoulders clipped a dark swath beneath the stars. I watched them as my eyes watered.

My brother Ben would have pointed out it's important to feel the place you are. *Now you do*, he would have said. And then he would have extended his wide hand.

With three fractured ribs and one gun-shot mattress the summation of my Montanan accomplishments, I spotted the poster stapled to a telephone pole outside of Red's Bar promoting an information assembly for Jeff Krystoff's grizzly bear tracking study. I realized it was do or die time, and I had to at least listen to Krystoff talk about the project in the relative obscurity of community attendance.

From my view in the back row of the assembly hall, Krystoff appeared to be masquerading as a grizzly in training, woolly beard and unkempt hair, an odd manner of pacing back and forth as if leery of the humans observing him. His eyes shifted from his pacing feet to the ceiling.

"Historically, we mostly studied griz by setting up culvert traps, filling projectile darts with Sucostrin and shooting them with compression guns. We brought them to their knees for the ten minutes or so it takes to strap them into wide collars with small transmitters and seven-cell battery packs, antennae loop wrapped in fiberglass cloth and caked in resin. Lovely little tracking cells so perfectly constructed, you'd think we were hoping to attach them to Christ's disciples.

"We'd take turns driving Ford Econoline vans at the perimeter of the wilderness area, vans equipped with stacked yagi antennae and map coordination equipment purchased from the Missoula airport. Pairs of study participants charted electronic blips, triangulated coordinates of study-collared bears, in fifteen minute intervals, across large swaths of Glacier and Yellowstone. We tracked bear activity through forty eight-hour blocks. We smoked a lot of cigarettes. Ate a lot of gorp."

Krystoff appeared mildly amused when his audience chortled.

"We also learned a lot about bears that way, how they migrate and what their sleep patterns are and so forth. But I'm interested in, I don't know, steering the van in another direction. What if all we really need is a trace of DNA, snagged in barbed wire? I want to see how far mere retrieval of hair samples will bring us. Something new, easier on the bears."

At this, Krystoff paused and looked out at the haphazardly strewn, largely chamois-shirted audience. He retold a meeting from the previous day where he was challenged by a critic who stated the downgrade in study invasiveness was a cop-out to mollify tree huggers and liberal academics. "It's bullshit," he said. "Science is progressive. It's supposed to work that way – you need less to do more. But no matter how you try explaining that, there's always a handful of morons with bruised egos and impaired imaginations who believe the only path toward new environmental awareness is roping, blindfolding and tackling your study subject to the ground. Seriously, what sense does that shit make?"

Krystoff explained further why he had been generating a new grizzly bear research study, how it relied on genetic technology and the collection of bear hair samples in place of radio-collared bears, and why he had chosen the Scapegoat Wilderness, east of Missoula, as the location he'd initiate it.

He ended his lecture by showing slide images he had captured of grizzlies in various Montana locales during his long years of research: massive, humped shouldered mammals with coats ranging from blonde to mud.

He explained how grizzlies can reach nearly one thousand pounds in a suitable habitat; how their musculature and vascular system, massive hearts, made them difficult to subdue in the days before high powered artillery; how their jaws hinged with two powerful muscles, a jaw capable of grinding any meal, even bone, into grit.

Intermittently pulsing the slide carrousel through its cache of bear images and flicking cigarette ash into a small pool on the concrete floor, Krystoff explained how grizzlies could rotate their forearms and use their front claws like fingers.

"We're talking majestic god-damned creatures, here," he said and smiled.

After the slide show, most of the audience shuffled out the door, back into the Missoula sunlight. I waited out the few that remained to ask Krystoff questions and then approached him to introduce myself.

"I thought we lost you," said Krystoff. He eyed me with a half smile. "Last check, the route from Minneapolis to Missoula is Interstate 94 with one entrance and one exit. But what the hell, maybe that's a cartographer's simplicity."

"I realize I'm getting to you later than we agreed on."

"You've missed the pre-training sessions."

"I know. I'm sorry for that."

"What did you say your major was, again? Biology?"

"No," I answered. "As I explained in my letter, I'm taking time away from school."

"Right." He took a long drag on his clenched cigarette, squinted, held it a moment and then exhaled. He looked me in the eyes. "And why bears, again? Remind me. What's your story?"

"I'm just very interested."

"You have any science study background?"

"Not formal."

He flicked his cigarette once. He waited. Then he flicked it again.

"Are there any warrants with your name in them? I have to ask."

"I've become extremely drawn to them in the past year or so," I said. "Bears, I mean. I don't have any significant science education, and I'm not even enrolled in non-science academics at the moment. I'm obsessed with bears. I've spent the past twelve months reading every book I could get my hands on, every article, including those you've written. On a daily basis, these animals have been roaming my thoughts and sleep for over a year. I came here to figure out why."

"Oh yeah," he smiled. "You're the dude that's been dreaming bear."

"When we talked on the phone, you said you were looking to add some non-biology majors to your group of volunteers."

"That's part of the plan," he answered. "The more this thing looks and smells like a community-based initiative, the better. It clears a path to a wider swath of funding."

"So you think you still might need my help?"

Krystoff paused, took a long drag off the smoldered ruins of the cigarette. "About these dreams you're having," he said. "You're not eating bear, are you?"

"Eating them?"

"Cutting them into pieces, sticking the pieces in your mouth and chewing them into your stomach."

"Bear?"

"People do."

"Fuck no," I said.

"The way to stop those kinds of dreams is to stop eating bear," Krystoff answered.

I waited a moment, let his advice dissolve. "I guarantee you, even as the very last option of survival, I am incapable of eating or marring a single ounce of bear."

Krystoff smiled, nodded. I had a feeling I may have passed whatever test he was giving me. That, or I was amusing him by going along with his inquisition.

"We're heading to the Scapegoat this weekend," he said. "It'll be a test run of the research equipment, study modality training, etcetera. I'm taking eight volunteers. Show up at 4 a.m. Saturday morning in the Citgo parking lot, if you are serious about being one of them."

And with that, he wrenched his slide carousel from the assembly hall projector, stashed it under his arm and sauntered out the double doors in a trail of curling smoke.

I was in.

At 3:45 a.m., the Citgo parking lot was barren, the sky wet ink, riddled with stars. Late August, there was a snap of chill in the air at that hour;

you could see your breath, and Missoula smelled of milled wood.

Before the other grizzly research volunteers showed up, I wondered if I had the right gas station.

And then they arrived, barely awake, in singles and pairs. Each resembled college biology students – blue jeans, fleece, some with long hair and ponytails. They chugged coffee. One flicked cigarette ash on the toes of his hiking boots.

We nodded to one another, mumbled hellos. It was clear the others were familiar with each other. I was the only new recruit.

Krystoff showed up last. In a shroud of smoke, he stepped from the exhaust-rattling white Ford Econoline van he left idling in the wan pool of light beneath the Citgo sign.

His fist in the air, he counted eight heads of volunteers and grinned. "Folks," he said. "We have a quorum!"

He threw Jesse, one of the volunteer leaders, a set of keys to the other Econoline van parked on the side street, and within minutes we separated into the two vans. We drove our duo van convoy along the freeway east and then State Road 20 to Lincoln, banked north, and, eventually, down the winding dirt and gravel trail that brought us to the chin of the Scapegoat Wilderness. It was wide spread of land, a quarter million acres of scarred moraine, a rugged mix of limestone cliffs, alpine meadows, wooded hillsides and timbered river bottoms. At the heart, was the Scapegoat Massif, an enormous, severe plateau surrounded by sheer cliffs, peaked at 9,200 feet, home to mountain goats, circling golden eagles, and wind-carved rock.

It was all beautiful. And strange. More than any other place I'd journeyed since stepping foot in Montana, I felt, from my corner seat of the crammed van, as though I was about to touch foot on the far surface of the moon.

We drove past a stretch of scorched browse and trees, hardwoods stripped of leaves, conifer thinned of needles – black, sculpted twists of wood reaching into sky.

"A fire swept the floor of the entire Canyon Creek valley last year," shouted Krystoff. He turned from the driver's seat, his first words since our van left Missoula. "Pretty much burned everything clean to its roots this entire corridor to your right."

It looked eerie through our windows this early in the day, the sky barely lit and the charred Lodgepole pine and larch, soaked in creosote, resembled Halloween scarecrows reaching for clouds. It smelled of sulfur and burn. The soil had turned to soot.

Krystoff slowed the van and let it coast. He turned to us and beamed.

"Beautiful, isn't it?" A half-burned cigarette was clenched in the corner of his grin. "To others, devastated paradise. To us, it's endless new possibility."

Krystoff seemed so in love with the cremated terrain, you nearly concluded he was the one that struck the match.

"Though not all the way through, you'll see signs of this fire throughout the Scapegoat. It's one of the reasons I centered our study here. The fire damage, the increased pressure from development and roads – those things set this corridor apart from others for research potential. It's our job to figure out how the griz population is adapting to all of this."

Krystoff moved us forward in resumed silence, and I wondered if what we were thinking of accomplishing was even possible, forget about likely. Could we really fan ourselves out across this partly charred, partly densely wooded and seemingly endless wilderness and walk home with our pockets filled with single bear hair follicles? What the fuck made us believe we could do such a thing?

Nothing, not the scorched terrain of hell itself, could get in my way of finding out whether or not we could.

Krystoff, swallowed by a University of Montana Grizzlies football sweatshirt, sporting a seven-day growth beard, Michigan Wildcats baseball cap, with curly dark hair nested over the back collar of his sweatshirt, explained to us how to strand a single eighty-foot length of barbed wire fifty centimeters above ground and wrapped around three or more trees.

"Imagine yourselves griz cowboys creating mini corrals," he said. He demonstrated our assignment – piled an arm load of decayed wood at the center of a barbed wire "corral" and doused it with a liquid lure of cattle blood and fish oil. He filled a metal film canister with a fragment of wool and then squirted it with a plastic bottle of some other concoction that stunk of rotten eggs and skunk.

"Bear cologne," he said. "These little canisters of rot will draw bears to the snag sites in search of bear love. Hold your noses when you put these together. Don't get any on your clothes."

Krystoff and a few of the volunteers had already plotted prospective hair snagging locations on U.S. Forest Service maps of the Scapegoat, pink dots of ink noting probable migration patterns and available vegetation. We were directed to set as many of the stations as we could before day's end.

With detailed topo maps folded into quarters and armed with rolls of barbed wire and snag station supplies, Jesse, another student volunteer named Theresa, Krystoff, and I hiked along the North Fork Trailhead, and followed the Blackfoot River. We climbed the bluffs, and noted the large tracts of east-facing slopes untouched by fire, green and dense. But the entire face of the hill opposite was scorched to the roots. We imagined flames leap-frogging whole lee sides of the hills, as if in a childlike game of tag.

With day packs strapped to our shoulders, water belts wrapped around our waists, we searched for signs of bear: claw marks around trunks, upturned boulders. My heart felt as though it was finally orbiting something that could provide a sense of belonging. I found myself more in the moment, less in sadness over what came before my trek to Missoula.

We hiked the duration of daylight, and paused only for snacks of protein bars washed down with canteen water. After setting up a number of hair-snagging stations as a foursome, Jesse and I split off from Krystoff and Theresa, hoping to cover more ground now that we had the process down. Jesse was easily a better orienteering expert than I and did most of the compass and map readings.

Collectively, we must have set up more than twenty snag sites by the end of the day. On the way, we never unearthed a single sign of bear.

That night, we camped at Carmichael Cabin, a 1920s shelter located after a knee-deep wade across the Blackfoot. Through the night, the sky darkened to pitch, and I imagined our strands of barbed wire in the moonlight, blue and cold. I imagined footsteps of approaching bears, the mounds of decayed wood suddenly in view as the curious bears loomed closer. Their snouts wiggled in the air as the scent of rotted cow and fish led them forward.

We built a fire, boiled water and served up a kettle of smoky coffee. We split a medley of dehydrated meals, bags filled with steaming water and set aside to take shape, lumpy and uneven, but warm and delicious under the circumstances – pasta prima vera, mushroom stew, tomato couscous. Dessert was a quarter wedge apiece of apple and handful of graham crackers we each dunked into coffee. For the moment, we were kings.

The firelight winnowed shadows against our faces, flickered into the surrounding trees. We listened to Krystoff answer our questions about bears, maulings, and the potential danger of our study subject.

"Two women, different parts of the park, were mauled to death in Glacier the same night," he said. "One was a friend of mine. She was attacked by a griz that routinely fed from an open garbage dump in Granite Park Chalet. Glacier closed that dump. Not gradually. Cold turkey. Days later, two young women lost their lives. Same thing happened with the young man in Yellowstone. Closing a garbage dump on a park-conditioned bear is like roping an open bar off to a relapsed alcoholic – only a matter of time before someone's nose is bloodied."

We were silent. We listened to Krystoff discuss the times he had been charged by grizzly, the times his passage between them had crossed the line of danger.

"Your heart pretty much ends up in your throat or somewhere you can't even imagine it. These are fast animals. You have no idea. And they'll charge their prey a number of times so you have multiple chances to shit your pants."

Krystoff stood and gave us instructions on how to behave should a grizzly charge one of us.

"You want to look, you know – larger than they are," he said. "Extend your arms – try to double your perceived mass. Inflate your fucking ego – I mean, whatever it takes."

When he raised his hands in the air, fire-lit shadows trailed behind him. They climbed into the reaches of balsam.

"But whatever you do," he said, "don't run. You'll immediately look like a big, meaty jack-rabbit. Just freeze."

Theresa asked him if there was a point when you can tell the difference between a false charge and the real thing.

Krystoff smirked. He took a swig of the quart of chocolate milk he had been nursing all night, between sips of spirits.

"Their eyes sort of roll up into their lids," he said. "In the zone, as it were. When that happens, they've locked their target and have made up their mind. When the iris and pupils disappear, the bar tab is up. Nothing is going to change their mind. At that point, they're in it for keeps. You pretty much both are."

Krystoff instructed us not to attempt to decipher a false charge from the real thing.

"Don't take chances. If a grizzly is charging you, drop to the ground and tuck into a motherfucking fetus. If you have a god, pray to the son-of-a-bitch."

Krystoff tempered our imagined images of charging grizzly bears with assurances these animals have far more to fear of us than we do of them.

"You're going to put your life at a helluva lot more risk by pulling yourself from a bathtub than you ever will by walking through a bear filled woods," he said. "Four times your size, and they'll forge a mile out of their way to avoid contact. And in the million instances our paths and theirs cross, a handful, maybe, have resulted in violence against the human. I'm serious – a handful. Virtually none. It's almost always the other way around. But these are powerful animals, with their own rules about territory and dominance. They are other worlds, other nations. Take precaution. Use your head. If things turn badly, think about Jesus. There won't be time for loftier goals than that."

Krystoff went back to the business of nursing his quart of chocolate milk. We sat silent, stared into the fire, listened to the pop and hiss of burning pine.

My head swam a wide river of bear images. Each rush of wind through the trees became grizzly lumbering through the dark woods. They reared on their hind legs, twitched their wet noses. I pictured their thick heads, humped shoulders and their moonlight-washed coats.

The campfire popped and spit. The wavering bed of coals sent rolling spark flecked waves into the dark sky. The murmured voices of the others faded, and my eyelids grew heavy. I thought of Clare, and willed her to know the place in the woods I had found myself. And I dreamed of the soft soils and grassy meadows surrounding me, and the wet tongues of bears lapping huckleberries and mountain ash, elk thistle and white clover, yarrow, bistort and horsetail, the myriad of sedges and grasses these mysterious giants inhale from the earth while their footsteps tamp them to their roots.

The wind sifted through the high branches of trees, and I fell into the deepest sleep since crossing the Montana border – the deepest sleep I could remember.

From my sleeping bag on the floor of Carmichael Cabin, I watched the sky warm. Wind gathered strength through the trees, and the other study volunteers emerged from their sleeping bags. One by one, they shuffled off to the perimeter of the woods surrounding the cabin, peed, wiped sleep from their faces, cleared their morning voices, and murmured about newly discovered muscle aches and enthusiasm for the day.

Krystoff arranged the survey materials across the picnic table. He analyzed map coordinates. His expression revealed hope and fatigue. The rest of us set kindling over the campfire coals and re-ignited the fire. We set a kettle of water on the fire grate and waited for its hiss, a baggie of freeze dried coffee at the ready.

Krystoff ambled toward us, a toothbrush stabbed between his lips, his mouth foamy mint. He spat a small cloud at his feet.

"Ready to capture some ursus arctus hide?"

We sipped the last of our coffee near the fire, stretched the muscles that had knotted from yesterday's hiking. We cleaned the cabin site of all traces of our presence and doused the fire, and we geared up with study sample collection equipment – sterilized tweezers, lighters, coin envelopes, coordinate-inked maps, protractors, compass, and field books. Krystoff separated us into groups of two, again, each appointed to separate hair snag locations.

We were to gather as many hair samples and field notes as we could and find our way back to the vans by five p.m., sharp. We fanned out in separate directions, Theresa and I paired for the day.

The morning air smelled of conifer and the sour emulsion of scorched bark. It revealed itself a little more like Sleepy Hollow than Montana – moor-like fog, and the inky spires of charred trees.

The wind sent a soft whistle through the pine. It felt good just to be walking through woods, the only sound other than the wind our solitary footsteps, the occasional chirp of red squirrel and flushed grouse.

We walked a winding trail south of the cabin, followed a small, withered brook. Theresa helmed the map and compass after we both determined she had the better orienteering skills between the two of us – a challenge I had now lost twice in a row.

We remained alert. Our eyes scoured the trees for signs of bear claw marks or rubs.

When we came to our first hair snag station, the sun had just cleared the timberline. The stretched wire at the station was bare, no signs of bear. We continued on.

We unwrapped mocha flavored power bars and chewed. Our eyes darted from trees to clouds to the hovering kestrels. In the background, a creek sputtered and gurgled. I ran my hand over the velvet moss cloaking a cedar.

We walked on. Theresa checked the coordinates on her map against the compass, made sure we were on track. The sun held high above us now, the shadows of trees compacted. In the near-noon warmth, I tied my sweatshirt around my waist and felt perspiration prick my neck and chest.

We approached our thirteenth hair snag location, a small clearing yards from a creek, and immediately knew something was different about this one from the others – the lure-scented wood was strewn from its former nest. We approached slowly. Hope built in our chests.

"Something's been here," said Theresa.

Our gazes sped the length of barbed wire, and we simultaneously reached to point at the unmistakable strands of golden brown hair clutched between the barbed prongs – a dozen or so neat brown and silver strands.

"Holy shit," we said in unison.

We located hair in about half a dozen barbs and carefully removed each strand with sterilized tweezers and placed them in small paper envelopes. We marked the collection envelopes and placed them in desiccation chambers. We doused the barbs with the flame of a lighter, erased the remaining traces of DNA.

We re-built the wood pile, both of us amused by the logs scattered like a child's tantrum.

"Can this really work?" I asked. "I mean, can you really gather samples like these and do something with them? Weave together some kind of real story with these tiny strands of hair?"

I held the parchment envelope toward the sun.

"Sure as shit," answered Theresa. "It's a relatively new technique, but you'd be surprised."

Theresa explained how the hair strands would be examined to isolate intact follicles. Samples that contain at least five follicles were washed in a solution that breaks down the protein surrounding the DNA. She explained how DNA analysis would determine the species, unique identity of the bear, gender and genetic relationship from one individual to others in the same wilderness corridor.

"Pretty soon," she said, "we'll know everything about the bear with simple chemical analysis."

"Name, rank, and serial number."

"Favorite coffee house, political affiliation, sexual orientation, S.A.T. scores..."

By 4 p.m., Theresa and I had visited twenty-seven hair snag stations and were successful at collecting samples from just the one. Still, we had the one. We chatted incessantly on our return to the van. Adrenaline flowed from our immersion both into wilderness and the beginning of a promising study.

I asked Theresa if she had worked with Krystoff before.

"First time with grizzlies," she answered. "I helped him with a nocturnal coyote tracking study last year. Bears though – that's his specialty."

"I've read that," I said.

Theresa told a story legend among the other volunteers – about a grizzly cub Krystoff observed fall out of a tree and lose consciousness when it struck the ground. From a cluster of aspen and through his binoculars, he watched the cub's chest. Detecting no movement, Krystoff bounded through the clearing, unconcerned over whether or not a sow griz hid in the periphery. When he got to the cub, he took a moment to check its vitals – heartbeat, breathing, pupil dilation, all checked in rapid succession. He leaned in, wrapped his fingers around the cub's whiskered muzzle, opened his mouth wide, kissed his lips against the bear's and exhaled, filled the young bear's lungs with his own breath. He repeated the sequence a half dozen times, and the cub's front paws batted the air.

It was all I needed to know about Krystoff – the only reassurance I needed to follow him at whatever human distance he'd allow.

"There are bears here," I told Clare. I phoned her as soon as I came through my apartment door. "Boxcars full of them. Grizzlies. Golden-haired and roaming through woods and ravines."

"Good," said Clare. "We knew that, though, right?"

"Now we have proof! Single strands of griz hair wedged between the metal barbs of wire. I held them between my own fingers, Clare. Grizzly hair strands!"

I hurried through my description of my first weekend in the woods. It was the first time in some while I found myself exhilarated, brimming with details.

After she listened to me re-tell the tracking weekend a second time, I asked her about hers.

"Oh, you know," she said. "Most of it spent with my nose pressed in books."

Clare asked me for details on the schedule of the study, how long it would last.

"Depends on the weather," I told her. "We're hoping at least for two more months of field research before winter. Trouble is, it's every other weekend. But, I told Krystoff I had all this time and wondered if I couldn't help him on the weekends when he drives out there solo to improve the stations."

"You like him, then," said Clare.

"From what I can tell, he lives and breathes this stuff."

I told Clare the story of Krystoff placing his mouth over a heart-stopped bear cub's lips to breathe the young animal back to life.

"He's a bit of a puzzle. Hard to figure out," I added.

"Two peas," she said. "One pod."

"But I think this study might be the very thing I need to, you know, figure out my – "

"Obsession?"

"Okay – I was reaching for a more positive word, but obsession works. I guess."

"It really is good, Jack," she said. "I'm happy for you. Relieved, too. You sound more…like yourself."

I wondered if Clare continuously wrestled with the doubt I'd find my way back to the person she remembered before I lost my brother.

"Are you planning on staying there past fall, then?" she asked.

"You're thinking I shouldn't be?"

"I'm wondering. I mean, if the study goes dormant in just a couple months – "

"There's the research to compile, and even though I won't probably add much to that, the hope is the field work will start back up in April, May at the latest." I added, "Aren't you still planning on grad school here?"

"I hadn't cancelled those plans or anything," she said. "You said you only had a couple months of study left this season, and – "

"It's only the start of what I came out to explore, though."

"And you've been so homesick out there."

"I have. Clare, this weekend I plucked single strands of grizzly hair from barbed wire I had strung the night before. Single strands of hair that weren't there the day before when I stood in the exact same spot. I held them between my own eyes and the sky."

"That's good, Jack. That's so good," she said, and she sounded as though she was struggling with how to feel about it – whether to celebrate or question. "I've just, I don't know, spent a little time wondering if we're doing the right thing at the right time – moving in together and everything. I want us to make sure we do it the right way. Before I pack up my life and move it all the way out there. Before we sit across from one another in wonder, you know, how two people in a relationship are supposed to communicate."

"That's what we're doing," I said. "I need you here."

"And that, Jack – " she said. "That's the other thing I've been wondering about." She trailed off. "I want to make sure, really sure, we have a life together when I get out there. Like we did before losing Ben. One that's growing...moving forward. You know?"

"I thought moving in together was what you wanted, and – "

"More than moving in together. And more than me taking care of you, or taking care of myself, while you disappear in some new stretch of wood."

At that, we both fell silent. I imagined myself traversing through holes in the clouds, my blue, naked body reaching backwards for Clare's missed grasp, her long hair veiling her expression.

"There has been that," I said.

"These bears, this weekend," she said. "Did you actually get to see any of them?"

"Only their hair. Single strands, not stitched together into whole bear."

"When you do see them, and I know you will, Jack – when you see them actually move through woods, in front of you. When you finally see them in the world – will that be the proof you need to resolve your brother's death and all these bears following you?"

I suppose Clare was asking me the simplest of questions, wondering if there was an end goal, mulling aloud the possibility of healing. How could I break the news to her resolution was, as yet, the farthest concept from my thoughts?

"I really don't know," I told her. "Everything is day by day, bear by bear, right now. You act is if I have any idea what direction this is heading."

From my weekend in the woods, I could still feel the imprint of warm sun against the back of my neck.

part two

.

In his world without weight, the diver orients himself to the strange behavior of inanimate objects.

Jacques-Yves Cousteau, The Silent World

MINUTES BEFORE MIDNIGHT OF CHRISTMAS Eve, Clare pounded her gloved fist against the door of what was, up until that moment, my unshared Missoula residence. She clutched a convenience-store-purchased sprig of mistletoe, steepled her arm above her head, and said, "And goodwill toward men."

She beamed. Her plump cheeks were red, her scarf tucked beneath her chin.

"I hit snow in the pass between Butte to Deer Lodge," she said, and unraveled her scarf. "I thought I was going to have to pull my car over and spend the night, or find a free manger somewhere."

"You should have called me to let me know," I said. I took her coat.

"I didn't see a phone. Like anywhere. I figured if I didn't make it here by morning you'd know to send the Cavalry. Does Montana own a Cavalry? What is a Cavalry?"

It was more than good to see her. The first time in months, and all this way, states from home, here on Christmas Eve. My heart pounded. Her hair was longer, softer at the shoulders, her pretty green eyes lit and searching. In an instant, I was reminded how much I missed her.

"Can you spare a cup of Christmas tea?" she asked. She plunked herself against my newly acquired pawn store sofa, and draped her arms along the back. "Oh my god. We live here, don't we?"

She said it as though it had finally crossed her mind after a twenty-two hour drive from her childhood home in Minnesota. She said it as though she had just realized she was more than just a little bit tied, now, to a completely new forwarding address.

Her eyes searched the room. "You were right about the decor," she said. "Very seventies. People sat in this apartment listening to ABBA, I'll bet. Lots of ABBA."

"It's pretty horrible," I said, and streamed water into a saucepan. "But the lease runs out in two, three months. We can look for something better. Together."

Clare's gaze absorbed the collection of images across the wall, the long line of black and white 8x10s of Clare twined in bedsheets, photos taken when her hair was cut short, our third summer together, then to a photo of Ben, Alex and me crowded around a sailboat wheel, steel wool clouds behind us, and then the Hamm's beer poster tacked to the wall, an advertisement featuring a soft-focused photo of a bearded, plaid-shirted gentleman with a docile grizzly bear walking along his side, the golden sun streaming across their shoulders in their joined walk through meadow, the words "Hamm's, the beer refreshing" beneath the image.

"Do I get to, you know, contribute? To the interior…design?"

"If you like it, we can keep it the way it is," I told her, and engulfed the stove burner in flame and set the saucepan of water over it.

"It's you," she said, smiling. "And I'm glad we're here, together. Regardless."

"I told you," I said. "Needs work. Everything here…needs work."

Clare traipsed into the kitchen as I steeped her tea.

"I'm famished, too," she told me. "Nursing a box of Cheez-its since Billings. This is no time to bogart the Christmas ham, is what I'm saying."

She parted the fridge door, spotted its gaping belly, save a single jar of mayonnaise, a carton of milk and a package of Tillamook cheddar.

"A full meal is going to be more challenging than tea," I told her. "Unfortunately."

She opened the cabinet door, counted the dozen or so boxes of mac and cheese.

"Jack and cheese," she said. "I think that's your new nickname."

"Or ours together," I said.

"But seriously, Jack. I am starving."

Later, as Clare devoured her second grilled cheese sandwich, after she inserted the toasted bread triangle between her lips, she took a long look at me. I'm sure I'd changed physically since she had last seen me – my hair tufted beneath my ears, against my collar, the three-week beard that peppered my face. It had been four months since we saw each other.

She leaned forward and kissed me, her lips salty from butter and cheese.

I pressed my thumb lightly along her cheek, through the light wisps of hair along her neck.

"It's so good to see you, Clare," I whispered.

"Oh Christ, that's good to hear," she whispered back. Her voice caught at the last word.

"Are you okay?"

"My heart is pounding with the collective force of the Blue Man Group. I can barely breathe straight."

"You're scared?" I asked.

"Like you wouldn't believe," she answered. She leaned into me and whispered. "I've got all my stuff boxed up out in my car. I'm a thousand miles from home. And I want so much to believe this is the right thing for us. After all this time, I want so much for this to be a good thing. For each of us. And us together."

"A good thing is all I want this to be, too," I answered. I leaned my neck against her breath, and ran my hand between her shoulder blades, where I imagined tiny, flowered buds branching into large, hourglass membranes that clasped and separated.

Clare's eyes moved back and forth beneath their lids. I watched them for nearly an hour. I remained as still as I could and wondered what dreams scrolled across her subconscious: images of the home she left behind, moments of our early love, fragments of memory I had yet to hear about – Clare's ever teeming world of hidden thoughts.

After all our time apart, off and on for nearly two years, Clare was finally alongside me, our naked bodies warming each other's, our two lives more permanently attached to a shared life than they had known in some time – my wayward quest the breath of bears, her less wayward one graduate geography studies, her separation from home, the restoration of a wounded love and maybe a thousand more causes I could only guess at.

I wanted to spread my hand across her warm chest, feel the expansion of her lungs, the swell of her heart, feel the evidence she was real. Instead, I watched her breathing, and the illuminated numbers of her alarm clock pulsing intermittent shapes over her beautiful shoulder. And I wondered what would happen to us.

The first few weeks of Clare's arrival were like a landing on the moon, as if we both walked from room to room in space suits, as though orphaned spoons and pens pinged off the ceiling, our bodies and all objects surrounding them weightless and strange. In the

mundane choreography of our lives, we barely recognized ourselves
or each other.

Clare opened her belongings; sealed boxes lined along the wall,
split open at the rate of one per day. Each object pulled free was set
immediately on her lap, contemplated and then set in a new place
or wrapped back up and set aside.

She was quiet. She barely ate at meals. She took her time getting
dressed, sat in long baths until the water turned cool, would join me
for tours of the city and surrounding area in abbreviated outings.

As was Clare's way, she mostly kept her thoughts to herself – tried,
instead, to brave a smile. But her embrace was softer, more wan, than
I ever remembered it. Often she slept twelve hours straight.

I drove Clare north, past Polson and around the perimeter of Flathead Lake. When I first arrived in Montana, the oblong, tree-lined
body of water reminded me of home, of Minnesota lakes, and I
thought it might her, too.

She was silent as we drove. The sunlight through trees flickered
across her face and lap, her head tilted toward her window. But in
the intermittent flashes of reflected sun against the glass, I could see
her smile. She stared out across the choppy water.

We parked my truck and walked into the Flathead National
Forest, a long meandering trail that led us through the shadows of
tamarack, larch and pine. Our boots stitched new tracks through a
newly fallen dusting of snow.

We watched a pine marten chase across an opening of the trees
and run the height of a birch and disappear into a woodpecker hole
gnawed into the wood.

Clare barely said a word along our walk, her steps close behind
mine. Every once in a while, she placed her hand inside mine and we
walked together. When she let go, she thrust her gloved hands deep

into her coat pockets and stared at the trail before us.

"Holy god, remind me how all this works," she said, and turned into my chest, hid her presence, momentarily, from the other guests. In Clare's hand, a glistening, bacon-wrapped water chestnut speared through its center by a yellow toothpick was blanketed in a green cocktail napkin.

"Drinks would probably be a good first move," I told her.

"Get as many as you can hold," she said. "And meet me in the stairway."

I was nearly as nervous as Clare. I had avoided social gatherings for as long as I could now remember, my treks through the Scapegoat with the other bear volunteer researchers the closest I'd come in some time to the sport of mingling. But this room was filled with Clare's new peers, fellow University geography grad students and faculty, every one of them strangers yet to her, except by face. Clare had been engaged in the program all of one week. This, the first event, a post New Year's party, she had been invited to since joining the program mid-year. Her heart had drummed so soundly on our way up the walk, I could hear its tremor in her voice.

The sink in the kitchen brimmed with ice cubes and beer bottles, and I pulled two bottles free and poured a plastic cup of vodka and then maneuvered my way back through the party throng, toward the stairway. I grasped the drinks in my hands and nodded to strangers with a half smile. I spotted the top of Clare's brunette head and moved towards her.

"This won't be nearly enough, will it?" she asked. She inhaled the cup of vodka in a single swallow.

"Not like that, it won't," I said.

We sipped the beers, and Clare attempted to identify for me the students and faculty she knew, at least, by appearance.

"That's the girl I told you about who fell asleep in spatial analysis – the first class. The one whose text book fell off her desk and woke her up in a shudder."

Clare's eyes darted across the room. A trace of perspiration dampened her forehead. I kissed her neck and felt the warmth.

"What's somersaulting across the mat in that head of yours, anyway?" I asked her.

She peered around the room.

"How many matches it would take to set this house on fire and get everyone out safely," she said, "including the artwork, so we can simply have the memory of a shared event."

"But also have it over with?" I asked.

"Pretty much, yes," she said.

When I returned from the kitchen a second time from having secured us more alcohol, I lost my way back to Clare, lost her in the crowd. She had left the hold of the stairway when others had moved in. And then I spotted her across the room where she leaned her hip against the arm of a sofa and distracted herself by looking at a long line of framed portraits along the wall.

In that moment, I was brought all the way back to the first time I saw her, a beautiful new face across a crowded room. She was dressed unlike anyone else in the room, in her black skirt and mustard-colored tights, bangles down her arm, matte lipstick and eye shadow the color of soft bruises.

She was the same open eyed young woman – equal proportions of warmth, mystery and luminosity – the same girl who entered the room, years ago, and forever changed my life. She was the same, only older.

I wondered if this wasn't the place our new beginning could finally root — the exact geographic or spiritual or chronological setting we needed to start over, to set our feet alongside each other's and move, together, in the singular direction we both silently longed for but had closed our eyes and missed. *If not here, where?*

She bit her lip sideways, leaned against the sofa, and tapped her foot to Kurt Cobain growling about feeling stupid and contagious, her legs crossed at the knee. When she finally spotted me, she smiled, mouthed a "hi, you" across the room, and I moved past the bent elbows and drinks clasped in cocktail napkins. When I got close enough, she leaned into me and plucked one of the glasses of iced bourbon from my hands.

"It's like I forgot how to be the new recruit, you know? How to expose myself," she said, and smiled. She leaned into her first sip of the bourbon.

"You just have to forget the things you're afraid of," I said. "You're all here for the same reason. I'm the one that doesn't belong."

We sipped our bourbon. Our hands found their way into one another's. We watched the party from the periphery.

"You should mingle," I told her. "Meet these people."

"Or maybe we should take a drive instead," she said.

She squeezed my hand.

"Remember that place you said you drove the night you got here?" she asked.

"That was Pattee Canyon Drive," I told her.

"With all the stars and cows."

"All of them," I said, and smiled at her.

"Maybe you should drive us there," she said, and leaned into me.

"It's also the place my mattress was shot."

"Oh, yeah," she said, and giggled. "I forgot about the shotgun baptism."

"These are the people you said you needed to start getting to know," I said.

"I will. Just not yet. I want to see the way this place looked the first night you arrived, when I was all the way back in Minnesota and you were trying to figure out if coming here was, you know, the right thing."

Her eyes were glossy, dazzling.

We banked the canyon, the winding dark road, and Clare slipped carefully out of her tights. I kept my eyes mostly on the road, but I sensed her movement. She slipped off each shoe, wiggled free from the waist of her tights, pulled the clinging fabric slowly, evenly down her legs, peeled it from her shins, bunched it into her palm at the ankles and removed each foot. She slid her underwear down her legs.

We coasted the same stretch of road I had discovered that first night, the one that overlooked the city lights. The same cows sauntered across the moonlit field. I imagined a singed kiss of gun-powdered earth somewhere in the darkened soil, my mattress ticking seared into the earth where the manic landowner had shot through its center. I wondered whether the timothy and brome had begun to green over the scorched pasture.

When I turned the ignition, we watched each other in the darkness. She was beautiful and strange at once, like someone I completely understood and still barely knew, and I wanted more than anything to fall into her and lose my way back.

I held her close, felt her warmth press against me, felt her shoulder blades through the sport coat I had draped over her shoulders when we left the party. I slid my hand beneath it, across her warm skin, and pressed. I fell into her kiss, and her mouth was sweet from the bourbon.

We held each other, and her hair fell across her face. I watched her purple shadowed eyes shut, her mouth part, and her expression shift – past our presence together into a new and distant place of her own.

For a beautiful moment, I lost track of where we were. I'm pretty sure we both did. It felt as though nothing had changed.

"We were walking through a sea of sawtooth grass," I told her. "It was just the two of us surrounded by all this shallow water."

Clare nodded. She was wearing blue and gray flecked flannel pajama bottoms and a silk camisole, her hair gathered behind her head and folded upwards into a pretty spire.

"We were walking this narrow isthmus of swaying green, both of us barefoot. Our hands separated when we both tried to secure solid footing. We were both afraid we'd sink into the cold sloughs.

"And then it took me a minute to get my bearings. I didn't see you anywhere, and I had this feeling you had slipped beneath the water."

Clare listened attentively, her knees tucked into her chest. The soft morning light spread its warm palm across her shoulders. Of anyone I knew, she listened most carefully to the details of recounted dreams, especially mine.

"So, I searched the tidal pools surrounding me until I spotted you. You were completely submerged. Your hair draped across your face sort of seaweed like. I was frustrated I couldn't see your expression, couldn't find your eyes.

"I reached my hands deep into the water, wrapped my fingers around both your wrists and tried pulling you toward me. But you pulled back against me and we struggled, and when your face finally broke the surface, I kept asking you why you were resisting, why you couldn't let me pull you free."

"Why couldn't I?" Clare asked.

"You told me my hands didn't feel like mine. You didn't recognize the feel of them. You said they were rough and they weren't mine, even though I thrust my arms before you and asked you to follow the fingers to palms to wrists to forearms to bicep to shoulder to neck to chest. I kept telling you it was the same me, only different, only a little bit changed and new."

"In this dream," Clare asked. "Were you *you*, or were you a bear?"

"I think I was both," I told Clare.

Clare was quiet. I watched her swallow.

"So, in this dream, did the you in the dream understand why I resisted?" she asked.

"Not really," I told her. "I kept thinking you ought to know it was still me. You ought to trust me enough to let me pull you free. If anything, I wanted you to know, as a bear, I was even stronger than before. And you were safer because of it."

"Because you were part bear?"

"Yes," I answered. "Why else?"

Entering Krystoff's office was the academic equivalent of approaching a bear's den: shelves of leaning books blocked the light, and the tile floor was blanketed in a centimeter thick dusting of cigarette ash in an oblong apron surrounding his chair. His desk was covered in sheaves of papers in between rocks and the bones of a reconstructed rodent, the lower jaw of a grizzly, its pointed canine teeth like football goalposts that framed a neat row of chipped incisors; an old metal tuna can punctured and gorged, presumably, from a similar (if not the same) bear's jaw; a dog-eared forest service poster of Smokey the Bear, his head shadowed beneath the wide brim of a ranger hat, the words "Only you…" centered across the poster's lower fourth. When you walked in, a swirl of cigarette ash parted under your steps and then hung lazily in the shaft of sunlight through Krystoff's campus-facing window.

"Most of the lab work is in," he said, pleased that the first leg of his new study was behind him. "It's good, Jack. Nearly two dozen individual bears fingerprinted and cross referenced."

"Is that significant?" I asked. "What you were hoping for?"

"Significant stuff," he answered. "Damned straight it is. We spent what, all of two and a half months up there, and we've got enough research compiled to show what bears are there. We'll be able to estimate the population, the overlapping home ranges, maybe throughout the Northern Continental Divide ecosystem. We can start to trend survival rates and identify coordinates separating populations. All of this, Jack, through hair follicles carried home in paper envelopes, our valued sacraments. Mother-fucking right, it's significant stuff. Nobody's done this, any of this, before."

Krystoff angled his quart of chocolate milk toward his chin, took a long chug and wiped the back of his hand across his lips. Chocolate froth clung to his beard and mustache. "The best part, Jack? We gathered all this data without a single blow dart, not one junkie griz in our research bucket. Not one airplane with telemetry equipment passing overhead and driving the study subjects into the god damned trees."

I smiled. I wanted to tell Krystoff I was happy for him, happy to be a part of his study. I wouldn't admit how the results of the study mattered to me less than simply seeing a bear. Just one.

"I'm still envious so many of the other volunteers got to see one, and I never did," I told him.

"You'll get your chance," he said, and engulfed a fresh Winston in flame. "The spring migration is a whole different ball of wax. They emerge from their dens as shaggy as hungover freshmen. They stagger into open fields and bow their heads and fill their mouths with pretty much anything blooming – dogtooth violet seed pods, yellow bell – shit like that. It's a whole different buffet line."

"The salad days," I said.

"Exactly that," Krystoff smiled. "Open meadow days. It's difficult not to see them when they swagger across flats in search of sedge roots."

I imagined grizzlies shuffling across wide fields, dazed from winter, their fogged breath like flowers in the early April sun.

"I miss it," I told Krystoff. I moved to his doorway. "I'm finding it painful to wait until spring."

"Don't then," he said. "You won't find bears, but there's nothing stopping you from learning the Scapegoat in winter. Could help you make your way around it even more adeptly come thaw."

"My girlfriend is here, now," I told him. "She already worries I'm turning into one of our research subjects."

That's when Krystoff told me of the legendary myth from the Haida culture of British Columbia, about the young woman who picks berries in the woods and is wooed by a handsome man who wears a bear skin cloak, how he draws her farther up the mountain until she forgets about returning home, how he digs a den for her in the fall, and reveals, eventually, his true nature of bear.

Krystoff engulfed a second cigarette and explained that the woman gives a winter birth to two children, half human and half bear. And that the woman's brothers find the den in the spring and kill her bear husband.

"She follows her brothers to the village with her two children," Krystoff said. "But, one day, one of her brothers cloaks her and the children in a bear skin, and they immediately turn into bears."

"And then what?"

"She kills her brothers and returns to the woods with her cubs."

"Christ, then..."

"Tricky business merging into bearhood," Krystoff smiled. "In some societies that harvest bear, the unmarried women are only allowed to eat the bear meat from the rump, never the front, especially not the front legs."

"Why not the front legs?" I asked.

"Think about it, Jack," smiled Krystoff. "You want to keep the community females from falling in with bears, you gotta keep them from the limbs that do the embracing."

Nearing the frayed edges of our collective savings, I sewed together a patchwork quilt of part-time jobs to help pay our $300 apartment rent and monthly grocery bill.

On weekends, I worked at Freddie's Feed and Read, a part organic food co-op and part independent bookstore. I took turns at the register ringing up Nietzsche and tabouli.

I worked a couple shifts a week at the campus ROTC gymnasium, checked student IDs and maintained the locker room and running track.

Weekday mornings at 5 a.m., I completed a newspaper route. I sliced open bulging stacks of *Missoulian* newspapers at the corner of our apartment building and hiked a spider pattern into the neighborhood, in the cobalt blood of pre-dawn, and tossed folded newspapers across moonlit lawns. My footsteps over concrete sidewalk were the slumbering neighborhood's only pulse.

We were living paycheck to paycheck, barely keeping our heads above the tide of our meager expenses. In between the scattered work hours, I made time for bears.

I still woke in the musky cowl of their breath. I was silent about it; I didn't want Clare to know I was still making my way through the long shadows of trees.

I woke when the light was still blue. I watched for the pulse along Clare's smooth neck, her softly clasped eyelids. I listened to the slow cadence of her breathing.

And then, I imagined the wind whistling through the crisp tendrils of reed grass, bleached into paper by wind and winter sun. I imagined myself burrowed beneath the roots of upturned spruce, the redolent earth. I waited, watched. Sometimes, I even imagined myself curled up in the open, my breath shallow, as I waited for the fall of snow to blanket my shoulders.

I had learned the trick of slowing my heart to single beats spread across whole minutes. I wondered if I couldn't also teach my body to convert nitrogen waste to protein, urea to creatine. *Could I learn the trick of bears staving off the loss of muscle and bone density across solid months of inactivity and starvation? Could I transform the whole of the human body through the miracle of bruin torpor?*

The wind whispered across the imagined snowy flat, whistled through the balsam. I watched the burled underbelly of winter clouds stretch their knots above our heads, lost in the beautiful darkness of the moonless world.

Early March, winter still blanketed much of the Bitterroot Range. The sky remained a concrete gray. We hardly saw the sun for weeks, and days alternated between darkness and flurries – long stretches of snowy sheets that trailed through the passes and valleys, and descended into the browse. Mostly, I watched it from our apartment bay window. In Missoula, the stench of the logging mill steeped the entire canyon days, weeks at a time, until the wind gathered strength and swept it away.

I left a note for Clare: "Need to see the Scapegoat. Homesick for it. Home for dinner."

I slipped on my thermal long underwear, wool Swedish army pants, fleece sweatshirt, down vest, and loaded a small backpack with granola bars, a thermos of hot cider, and a pair of binoculars. I got in my truck and drove east of Missoula, along Highway 200, and turned into the Scapegoat trailhead as the first trace of snow swept the gravel road through Klienschmidt Flat.

Flocked white from recent passing snows, the conifer were beautiful. The entire pass looked worlds different from my memory of it from fall, more like a snow globe holiday scene than the raw landscape formerly standing in its place.

With my Sorel boots laced to the top eyelets, I hiked through the flat bluffs that bordered the west bank of the North Fork. The trailhead had been hiked by others, hunters perhaps, in the days preceding, and the trail, with boot prints hash-marking the snow, was easy to follow.

Without thinking, I hiked for hours. The new snow nicked my face, and melted at contact. It felt good, open. The huff of my breath, the sound of my boots against snow, and the river water curling around boulders and banked bends were the only sounds. When I stopped to rest, my heart pounded like a mallet against the warm bones of my chest.

And then snow poured from the nimbostratus. Dense sheets of white swept through the passes and curled like airy waves along the high ridges of talus. That's when I should have turned around and traced my steps back along the trail. The sun was already descending; there were only a few hours left of light.

Instead, I became drawn to the winter horizon to the point of a warm daze.

I climbed the ridgeline, past the burned snags of trees. Loosened pebbles rang downslope from my boots, my feet locked in place one over the other. The falling snow was cold when it lit against the back of my neck.

Out of breath, I cleared the ridgeline and sat. My chest heaved.

Snow moved in waves across the wide drainage below. It winnowed over the palisades, over meadow, against the massive, rocky bulwark directly across from my perch.

I stared silently into the falling snow. The sky behind it had darkened.

I lowered myself down the scree. It was easy to find the remaining indents of my footsteps on the most recent leg of trail, but farther along, as the sky inhaled all remaining illumination of sun, the same tracks had disappeared in the new crests of snow. It didn't take long before I relinquished the goal of forward progress.

When I checked my watch, it was nearing 7 p.m. I pictured Clare pacing our apartment, wondering when I'd return, wondering if she should continue warming our dinner or go ahead and eat without me.

I kept an eye on Dobrota Creek, felt confident I could follow it to the confluence of the Blackfoot and still trace my way back to the trailhead, trail or no trail. But there would be the question of exposure – walking into the night, into the cold, and the risk of getting lost, farther away from a safe passage back through the woods.

Amazingly, I felt calm; I felt content. The woods, the snow through them, were the most beautiful things I'd seen in some time.

I hiked to a swale near a treeline; the snow was to my knees. I tore a trench into the bank and pushed the snow into a mound. When the mound was well over my shoulders, I tunneled into the lee end. I hollowed out a cavity the length of my body and carved a chamber. I pulled snow into my chest and then inched backwards and hauled it out. When the chamber was large enough for me to enter and turn, I continued to dig but used my feet to push the snow out.

I pulled myself through the tunnel like an otter, stripped branches from nearby balsam trees and set them on the chamber floor. I pierced a myriad of holes, the pattern of Ursa Major, through the snow roof with a long spear of dead poplar.

I knew Clare would worry. I knew she'd likely wonder through much of the night where I was and whether I was okay. But there was no way to get word to comfort her. In the strangest of ways, I felt closer to her, more in love with her and connected, these miles apart, than I had in some time.

I ate my remaining granola bar and watched the snow flit across the dark sky. I snaked into my snow shelter and lodged my pack against the opening behind me. I curled myself over the conifer boughs.

It didn't take long until my body ceased its shivering, my own trapped body heat having warmed the cell. It took even less time before I fell into a deep, sound sleep.

A sapphire haze swam through the ice walls; the dawn sun illuminated the dense webbing of ice crystals. My head throbbed. I should have warmed more water the night before and sipped it before I slept. The lone thermos of cider hadn't been enough to stave off mild dehydration. But when I pulled myself on my elbows through the tunnel and pushed the lodged backpack through the opening, the world spun a little less the more breaths I pulled into my chest. The cold wind stung my face.

The sun was low on the horizon, and the newly fallen snow was bright and thick in nearly every direction. Clearly, too, the temperature had fallen significantly after the snow, the changing of fronts, and I sensed the air temperature was single digits, subzero with the wind chill. Steam rose from the creek as though it were spilled broth. Thin leaves of knotweed and prairie star were painted in hoarfrost.

In the bright daylight, it didn't take long for me to find my way back to the trail. All former footprints were erased in the overnight snow, but I recognized the slope of the trail banking the river gorge and walked it easily, my stinging ears my only minor concern. Orienteering was much easier in morning light.

I knew Clare was at home in a panic over my overnight absence, and I felt haste to make my way out of the woods. But I still found myself slowing to observe a flat meadow where I spotted a soft hiccup of snow followed by the puncture of the pink ears and nose of a long-tailed weasel. The small animal arced and then plummeted; its long white body and ink-blotted tail knit the snow with serpent-like undulations.

I hiked the snowy field, and inserted two naked fingers into one of the weasel's snow-punctured tracks.

And then I dug my hands deep into the fresh snow and through the shelf of ice beneath it, all the way into the soft, airy thermal core at the base of a young poplar. The darker layers of bark at the base had been stripped neatly into tiny swatches of green and white flesh, the fractional indentations of deer mice.

I sat with my back against the base of the poplar, and imagined the world beneath the frozen surface stretched before me. For the first time in these woods, my imagination enveloped more than just bears breathing slow bursts of winter air from their lungs. I wondered about the whole universe alive beneath the subnivian zone I had heard Krystoff talk about, the teeming, frantic winter lives of mice, voles and shrews. I imagined the web of ice crystals, how they thawed in sun, froze overnight, and formed a dense, snow-packed dome, how they trapped the warmth of the soil. Its vapor sutured a newly constructed thermal world of tunnels small creatures ran, animals that built grass nests and burrowed beneath leaf mold in winter's spreading labyrinth, a wide world into which I wished I had a direct view.

I moved on, back toward the trail, hiked through a boreal spit of conifer, clusters of tall spruce and fir, and then spotted the smallest of birds, dead in the snow. I cupped the bird in my hands. It barely weighed more than air, its body frozen solid, black eye slits crusted with frost. The bird was delicate and small, a yellow crown with a slight orange patch down the center, a white stripe over its mask, a cream breast and darker wings flecked with white and yellow. I turned it carefully in my hands.

It was beautiful.

I looked for puncture wounds or blood. I saw no marks, no twist of bone or visible injury. The small bird seemed as pristine as a Christmas ornament, dead without apparent cause. There were no animal prints in the snow leading to or away from the place the bird's body had fallen, just the small kiss against snow, as though the bird had fallen dead from the clouds.

I clasped my hands around the bird's body and waited, as if the frozen bird's body would thaw like a winter insect revived by spring. But no such miracle took. The bird's body softened and thawed, and it merely became more limp than I had found it, its breast just as still.

I placed the dead bird into my vest pocket and continued my hike toward the trailhead. During the rest of the hike, my heart raced with new ideas.

Clare stared straight into the lifeless eyes of the dead bird in my cupped hands, and back into mine. She didn't unclasp her folded arms.

"And some girls crave diamonds and roses," she said.

"I found this bird, frozen in the snow, in a stand of spruce. Its body perfect, not a feather harmed."

"The condition of its feathers seems hardly its most pressing concern," she said, her expression unchanged.

Clare stood still. A diamond of sunlight stretched across the hardwood floor between us. Though past noon, she was still dressed in blue flannel pajama bottoms, thick wool socks and a University of Minnesota sweatshirt. It was clear she hadn't slept much through the night or rested much through morning. It was also clear she was holding me responsible.

"I can't figure out what killed it. It had to have happened after the snows passed. As though it dropped out of the sky frozen solid."

"That's pretty much the shape I expected to find you out in those woods, Jack. Some cartoon Xs in permanent ink across your eyelids."

I smiled. Clare wasn't ready to smile back.

I told her I was sorry, that the snow fell harder than I noticed, and with daylight dwindling, I chose what I thought was the safest response – to shelter myself until morning, knowing all the while getting word back to her was impossible.

"Why not at least call me when you got to Ovando this morning? That would have at least saved two more hours of needless worry."

In truth, there was little I could offer Clare to reverse the concern she had already spent. It was fruitless, I suppose, to expect her to share the same curiosity, especially under the circumstances, of my mystery dead bird.

I set the bird back in my down vest pocket.

For a while, we let silence swim between us. Clare wandered to the window, her back to me, and when she turned, I noticed two lines of tears moving toward her chin.

"It was an accident, Clare," I told her. "I had no idea there would be so much snow so quickly, or that I'd become lost. Isn't the important thing I found my way back?"

"Have you?" she asked. "The worst part of worrying about you all night was realizing how long I've already been waiting for you to return."

I watched her from across the room.

"Do you have any idea what that's like?" she asked. "To wait and wonder if someone you love – if he'll return…"

"You know I do," I said.

"You should," she said. "After Ben, if anyone should know what that's like, it should be you."

I was silent, and she struggled to choke out the words, her arms across her chest. "First that whole cruddy winter," she said. "And then the summer, and then fall. I followed you all the way here, not knowing in the least what I would find. And now another winter, you locked in your private, little awe."

"This winter, it's not the same as last winter – "

"I followed you all the way here with the one hope the rest of this was past us, that we could start again, resume somewhere close to where we left off. Or someplace new, even. It's to the point I don't care what it is we build, just – as long as we're building *some*thing."

"Aren't we?"

"So last night…I waited for you all night. Mostly wondering whether I'd see you again. And it made me realize just how long I've already been doing this. Waiting."

"I know," I said. "I get that."

"There's nothing wrong with you burying yourself a night in the woods." Clare's voice was soft. "I get that part of you. I even get the part of you that cups frozen, dead birds in your hands on your way home. But it's just – I'm starting to notice how much I want to explore my life and who I am, other than this girl that waits for you to figure out yours."

"Okay," I said. "Okay."

"I feel like I'm straddling two very separate worlds," she said. "And it's starting to feel a little impossible."

I remained still. I wondered if she had any idea how in love with her I had always been. I wanted to tell her I believed I was finding my way, all the way, back to her. I wanted to tell her that, but the thoughts in my head seemed as disconnected as falling snow.

If I could find a way to burrow a chamber into the soil and lead Clare through it, our soft, naked bodies furled around each other's through whole, moonless nights, our kisses duff and rainwater, I would. With every last ounce of my being, I would.

I moved toward her, silent. I reached for her hand. She let me take it, but it was slow to unfold in my own. I pressed my other thumb against the feathered breast of the nameless dead bird in my pocket. I searched for the slightest trace of heartbeat, a single pulse hidden deep beneath its feathers.

• • • • •

For Clare's sake, I removed the dead bird from her sight. I placed its small body, now limp, into a Ziploc sandwich bag and tucked it into the farthest corner of the freezer, hid it beneath a package of frozen peas and behind a cylindrical carton of vanilla ice cream.

My intent was virtuous – give Clare at least a few days save from worry, show her no more signs of my branching obsessions with bears or woods or fallen and glaciated birds.

I kissed her forehead and sat quietly in front of the television with her that evening. I leaned against her shoulder. We consumed our mounded bowls of macaroni and cheese and sliced tomatoes. The steam banked our silent faces.

She was quiet all evening. She still seemed hurt and in wonder. Perhaps to show a small sign of reconciliation, she held my hand, placed it in hers and clasped it. That was the extent of the gesture, and I greedily accepted it. I brushed my thumb slowly and repeatedly across the back of her hand.

Later that night, though, I lay awake. Clare's pretty, sleeping face was washed in moonlight beside me. I walked to the kitchen, to the low hum of the refrigerator, opened the freezer door and pulled my sealed and frozen bird from its corner berth. I pulled it from the bag and turned the frozen and feathered ingot in my hands.

"Are you going to be in the lab any time today?" I asked Krystoff, phoning him at his home number as soon as the morning sun lightened our windows.

"Sorry?"

"I found this dead bird I want to show you."

"A dead one?"

"From the Scapegoat."

"Jack, it's Sunday."

"Sometimes you work weekends," I said, pretending I knew it was Sunday morning all along.

"Bring it in tomorrow after 3. I'll be in my office. How is the Scapegoat?"

"Frozen."

"Including its birds."

"Apparently, yes."

"Bring it in. Let's take a look."

When I walked into Krystoff's office, dead bird in hand, he peered at me over the rims of his reading glasses, a half–mauled Red Haralson apple in his curled fingers. A drip of cider ran, unnoticed by him, the length of his arm.

"In walks the western woods warrior!" he said. "Carrion in hand."

I set the bird on his desk in between his scattered papers. Its beak duller now and slightly agape, it was still so beautiful, this small bird.

"It's a golden crowned kinglet," said Krystoff. He pushed sheaths of paper beneath its body and moved it gently beneath his desk lamp.

"I found it in the snow," I said. "It's body perfect. As though it had fallen from the clouds."

"Was it windy the night before, do you know? Stormy?" he asked.

"I suppose."

"Probably fell from its nest and froze to death."

I pictured a series of birds falling out of the loden sky, popping from branches like frigid firecrackers, the floor of the woods littered with frozen bird corpses.

"They fall out of their nests? You're sure it wasn't a victim of wayward migration or something?"

"No. They winter here."

I paused. "That's a funny way of wintering."

"These kinglets," he said, and turned the dead bird in his hands, thumbed its feathers forward. "Amazing creatures. The woods are chock full of them, but you hardly ever see them. Their tiny forms make them impossible to spot. They make these cocoon nests, standing room only, for their large broods. And the mother often builds second nests and hatches another brood while the father nurtures the first batch."

"Bird Mormons," I said. "With split custody."

"Collectively, they might release twenty chicks during nesting season. But their mortality is so high," continued Krystoff. "Something like 90% annually. They need to propagate that many chicks at a time to keep their tiny heads above the tide of winter."

I pictured kinglets falling from the winter sky and shattering like icicles.

"How these tiny birds survive freezing, 16-hour winter nights at all," said Krystoff. "I mean, take a look at it; it seems hardly prepared."

"Nor was it," I added.

"It's possible they huddle together in snow caves perched on conifer boughs, little suspended igloos. That's the latest thinking on how they survive arctic nights."

"So you're thinking a wind scattered this one's igloo perch, and it was unable to find another before freezing to death?"

"It's possible," he said. He turned it in his hands. "Such a pretty little bird."

It was the prettiest I had ever seen.

I was halfway through a Saturday afternoon shift at Freddy's Feed and Read when Clare, accompanied by one of her professors and two of her fellow grad students, pushed through the glass door, text books wedged beneath their arms, backpacks slung over their shoulders.

They set their texts at one of our corner tables. Clare shielded the late afternoon sunlight from her eyes. She talked incessantly with her new friends, and never glanced over her shoulder to see if I was working the counter.

I watched her from the fiction section where I pushed books in place from the pancake stack of them I had towered on my pushcart. I hadn't yet been introduced to the professor or fellow students, but surmised their identities from conversations Clare and I shared.

It was fun secretly watching her engaged in conversation, like watching someone I barely knew. She smiled and nodded at the others, leaned into the table conversation. She laughed at a shared story.

Clare dove into her backpack and removed her wallet. She turned quickly toward the deli counter, and her face flushed when she saw me standing behind it.

"Oh, my goodness," she said, her eyes nearly tearing. "I completely forgot this is one of your afternoons here."

"At your service," I said, and smiled.

"Okay, well, we're in for a round of falafel sandwiches. Two on whole wheat, two on white pita."

"Coming right up," I said, and rang up her order. "Seven sixteen."

She handed me two five-dollar bills.

"You need to come and say hi," she said. I poured change carefully into her palm. "It's Keith and Mol and Dr. Bashiri. We're running through our plans for that tourism research grant I told you about."

"Oh?"

"It's so funny seeing you like this," she said. Her face held its flush.

"I'll put the sandwiches together and stop over to say a quick hi,"

I told her, adding, "You're a very cute grad student."

I assembled four paper plates of falafel sandwiches, loaded the pita half-moons with crispy, deep-fried, mashed garbanzo bean rounds, diced tomato and slices of cucumber. I set two plastic tubs of tahini sauce on each plate. On Clare's plate, I set a trio of cucumber slices I had carved into hearts.

"This is Jack," said Clare. I set the plates in front of her classmates and professor. They each shook my hand and smiled. "I completely forgot he was working here today."

"Cool place to work," said Keith. He had a taut, perch leather face and eyelids the heft of catcher's mitts — features that made him appear at least a decade older than Clare and Molly.

"I'm also a paperboy," I answered, and Clare clutched her chest, laughed, and her face flushed a darker hue yet.

"Paperboy and bear tracker," said Keith.

"Something like that," I answered.

"It's more than that," said Clare. "Jack's taking part in a ground-breaking grizzly research project Jeff Krystoff is heading up. This past fall, they compiled the most comprehensive, non-invasive bear tracking research ever gathered in any single corridor."

"I've heard about this," inserted Dr. Bashiri. He nodded enthusiastically. "Krystoff's Scapegoat study! I'm envious. Were I a younger man, you can bet I'd be walking those mountain trails alongside you."

I smiled, touched by the professor's kind manners, touched, too, by Clare's effort to speak up for me, warranted or not, and only a little hurt by the gentle manner she had inconspicuously pulled her napkin over the lip of her plate to obscure the view of the heart-shaped cucumber slices I had set there for her.

"Well," I said. "I have books to shelve and chickpeas to mash."

"And Winnie the Pooh to track," added Keith, attempting to solicit a laugh from his lunch-mates.

I glanced his way, held eye contact a moment. "Yes, well..." I said.

"It's nice finally meeting you, Jack," nodded Dr. Bashiri. "I look forward to hearing more about the study."

I nodded and smiled, caught Clare's reddened face one last time before I turned. Her silent expression had briefly mushroomed into the look of a sad but genuine apology. I wasn't sure whether or not I owed the same. Mostly, I wondered the rest of the afternoon what she had done with those hidden, heart-shaped cucumber slices I had placed on her plate. I wondered if their cold flesh had ever made their way to her lips, either in full view of her lunch-mates or in the invisible moment of privacy. I fantasized her pressing them into her warm hand and carrying them across campus. I pictured her running her fingers over their curved ventricle chambers in the dim light of her office, smiling at the private touch, as the sun lowered between campus buildings. I pictured her setting one across her tongue and waiting for it to dissolve, a heart shaped imprint on the roof of her mouth.

For my heart's safety, I never asked Clare about the cucumber slices. It was such a little thing, but funny how the little things sway nimbly in the balance.

My naked hands buried into the snow, I felt as though I was opening the body of a new world, its warm veins the labyrinth of tunnels that branched beneath the snow pack, subnivian tunnels and chambers that steeped the lasting musk of earth.

I pulled the snow from the bases of trees and ran my fingers across the smallest of teeth marks indented into the soft cambium.

In the Carmichael Cabin, I spent whole afternoons observing the winter antics of freeloading deer mice. I listened to their drum against the walls, their tiny feet thumping out deer mice Morse code against the joists. I uprooted tiny caches of seeds tucked beneath the floorboards and in the corners of a box and the lining of a small assembly of hats and mittens in the cabin's closet, the hidden larders of rodents.

Against Clare's wishes, I extended my day hikes into the Scapegoat into 24-hour pilgrimages, sometimes longer. I came home cheeks flushed with excitement, a notebook full of new notes and observances. I spent the next few days in between my jobs, and chased explanations at the university library. I camped out in the Life Sciences wing and devoured biology texts and articles.

One sunny day, I found myself on my stomach, my body stretched over the mottled ice of a wide pond. I spotted what looked to be the dark, oval shapes of painted turtles. They moved across the pond bottom. They darted and hovered over the aquatic forest of waterweed and stargrass. And then I raced back to Missoula and pored over an article in *The Journal of Experimental Biology* that explained the process of anaerobic respiration. It detailed how painted turtles survived winter by pulling oxygen from decaying plant material and releasing carbonate from their shells and bones. The whole process, stretched across long, cold months, beneath a ceiling of ice, basically forced the turtle's skeleton to consume itself until the spring thaw provided the opportunity for regeneration – a sub-zero loofah scrub.

I learned how frogs made their way safely through the same frozen duration, how their cells transformed into ice, a mix of glycerol and glucose in the frog's blood that protected the membranes during the freeze and fended off ice formation from entering the interior of the frog's cells.

"And you merely thought its swim in summer pond water was the frog's most Olympic feat," I said to Clare. I followed her from the bedroom into living room and back again, my finger pressed between the pages of an amphibian biology text, Clare with a hair barrette in one hand and notebook in the other.

"But *this* swim," I told her, "this amazing swim of its own blood chemistry – I mean, we're talking the combined talent of Jesse Owens and Nadia Comaneci times ten."

She glanced at me with barely a smirk.

"It circulates adrenaline to the liver, activates enzymes which convert its glycogen to glucose."

I paused to double check the details.

"Yep, glycogen to glucose. Magic, presto – instant homemade froggy antifreeze."

"Pretty cool," Clare muttered.

"Yeah, it is; can you imagine?" I followed her into the bathroom and watched her reflection in the mirror, over her shoulder. She pulled her long hair into an s-shape behind her head and clamped the barrette teeth into its overlap.

"I have to get a term paper drafted tonight," she said. She clasped my arm briefly, and passed me. "And I have student tests to grade."

"This little frozen frog, Clare. It completely reshapes its body chemistry over a twelve-hour prep for winter. Its heart and blood flow seize, its entire life suspended until spring thaw."

Clare perched on the couch, drew her knees into her chest, her texts and bluebooks fanned in front of her on the coffee table.

"Can you imagine that kind of faith?" I asked. "In anything? It's Zen Buddhist."

"Don't tell me that's something you are going to try," she said, her expression firm.

"Buddhism?"

"You haven't the blood of frogs, Jack. The cells inside you, they'd implode if frozen. You know that, don't you?"

"I'm aware," I answered.

"The swim of glycerol and glucose," she continued, "not even with water wings, arm floats or swimmies could you train your blood to – "

"Perfectly aware."

"Good," she said. "You have a tendency to admire these feats to the extreme."

Hours later, I circled the starlit neighborhood in the cold yawn of 5 a.m., rifled folded newspapers into doorways and then drove quickly back into the Scapegoat while the sunlight warmed the sky.

I hiked to the perimeter of a frozen bog, its reed grass crisp with frost. I stood and imagined the ice-cubed bodies of frogs sunken below my feet, hopeful prayers in solid soil. More than anything, I wanted to pry one safely from the frosted earth, place it in the center of my palm, and blow my breath through my laced fingers until the frog's small, weightless body warmed. I wanted to feel its wristwatch ticking pulse within its throat, the lightest drum of its revived heart.

And then there – newly awake, the tiny amphibian in my cupped hand, its frozen eyelids suddenly parted, I would lean in and whisper a single question: *How in the hell do you do that?!*

Clare was anxious about the invitation one of her professors extended her – a small dinner party at the professor's house, with several of the same individuals I had met at Freddy's Feed and Read days earlier.

"I won't have a thing in common to discuss with a group of geography grad students," I told her. "You'd be better off without me there."

"It's only dinner," she said. "Please say you'll go. There will be other non-students there, significant others."

When we moved through the entryway of Dr. Bashiri's house, a scattering of Clare's classmates were sitting on the living room floor with their legs crossed: Molly, Paul and his wife Lauren, Keith. Zither music played through the stereo speakers, and we handed Dr. Bashiri a bottle of ten-dollar Cabernet. We chatted greetings with the others, and Clare's professor hauled our coats off to a side room.

I felt a trace of perspiration prick my forehead, and I wondered how long this dinner event would last, and if I would have anything to add to the conversation. Sitting in a half circle around the living room floor didn't promote a whole lot of breathing room.

Dr. Bashiri poured us neat glasses of Aragh-e Sagi, a strong Iranian vodka that burned a flowered flame into your chest at first swallow, and we each smiled mutely at one another after downing them in short order.

For a moment, I wondered whether I was an asset or deficit to Clare's place in this company, and I found myself wishing for a side door or window I could slip my way through unnoticed.

"You're the bear guy," Paul said, and smiled. His wife Lauren tapped him lightly on the knee.

"Sorry?" I asked.

"Aren't you the one that drove all the way out here to count bears in the woods?"

I nodded and calculated imagined steps toward the door.

"It's an important research project in the Scapegoat wilderness corridor," said Molly.

"Oh, no, I didn't mean – "

"It's totally cool," continued Molly. "I'm completely envious I'm not a part of it."

I glanced quickly at Clare. Her face was flushed.

"Oh, yeah," said Paul. "Did I make it sound silly, or something?"

"You didn't," I said.

Dr. Bashiri smiled from the corner of the room. "We should all be so lucky to move through the woods counting bears," he said.

"Maybe we could make that our post dinner activity," said Keith.

And here I was feeling thankful for a possible close to the topic.

"How many bears on South Higgins would you project?" he

asked. "Is there a bear abacus you guys use? Little rounded ears on each of the wooden pegs?"

I nodded, silent. Only my second time in his company, it was becoming trickier not to assume this guy held some unidentified grudge against me. Or the study. Or maybe I was reading it wrong.

"I absolutely meant no – " Paul interjected.

"None taken," I said. "Forget it. And yes, I am the guy that drove all the way here to count bears in the woods."

"And we're all glad you did," said Lauren. "Otherwise we wouldn't have Clare here."

Dr. Bashiri poured a new round of Aragh-e Sagi, and we lifted our shot glasses and drank a silent toast.

"It's good welcoming you all into my home," said Dr. Bashiri. He ushered Clare and me through a quick tour of his small house, the remaining guests presumably already having had the privilege. And if they hadn't, I didn't care. The reprieve, from Keith, at least, was welcome.

Bashiri took time showing us his study, walked us past framed photographs of his family, his parents and brothers and sister, a photo of his wife, since deceased, dark eyes and a gentle smile.

"How did she die?" I asked.

"Ovarian cancer," he said. "Twelve years now. Very sad. Very sad."

He walked us upstairs, past a colorful tapestry hung on a far wall and into a half-story bedroom with dormer windows where a large porcupine scuttled across the floor of an eight-foot wire cage, a few tree branches strewn across.

This I hadn't counted on – an Iranian Geography professor in the middle of Montana with a live porcupine thundering across his half-story alcove.

"Did I tell you about Dr. Bashiri's porcupine?" asked Clare.

"It's a detail I would have remembered," I answered.

"I found him struggling on a wooded trail two springs ago," said the professor. "I think he had fallen out of a tree."

Again with the tree falling mammals. First Krystoff's bear cub and now this caged porcupine. Could none of the tree-climbing mammals of Montana maintain the dexterity necessary to remain adequately treed? I mean, why go up there in the first place, then?

"I thought only drunk humans and koala fell out of trees," said Clare.

"It's quite common," answered Dr. Bashiri. "Something like forty percent of porcupine skeletons in museums are said to have fractures most likely sustained from tree falls."

"And that's not from museum directors shaking the trees until they fall out?" I asked.

I pictured a woodland floor an assemblage of disheveled porcupines, bears, squirrels, martens and raccoons, all liberated from the skyward limbs of trees, cartoon stars swimming their heads.

"This one was freshly fallen," continued Bashiri. "Stunned and injured. I took him home, fed him, watched over him, gave him a warm bed. Now he walks again, only crooked."

Clare smiled. "He's very handsome. If you ever need a porcupine sitter..." she said, and gestured to the two of us.

We returned to the living room and joined the semi circle on the professor's wide carpet. Dr. Bashiri brought us cups of yogurt mixed with chopped shallots and a small salad of diced cucumber, tomato, parsley and onion mixed in an olive oil, lemon juice and black pepper dressing. When we finished, he whisked our bowls and salad plates away and brought us steaming plates of fried eggplant simmered in tomato sauce, yellow peas, and onions over basmati rice.

The entire house smelled of sweet spices and steamed vegetables.

I managed to sequester the bottle of Cabernet we had brought, planted it directly behind us and continued to pour myself glasses in between conversation on tourism's impact on sustainable development and sidetrack discussions of Helena politics. I nodded and smiled. I nursed at the wine until the bottle was empty.

I leaned into Clare's ear. "There's a porcupine above our heads," I whispered.

She smiled and laughed lightly. "I know, dear," she said, and patted my leg.

"A barbed rodent is scurrying, right now, right here above our heads and these thin joists..." I whispered.

"So show us this trick of yours," said Keith. He gestured at me with his fingers wrapped around a bottle of Michelob. "This thing you do with your heart."

"Keith!" said Clare.

"His heart?" asked Paul.

"If it's not topical," said Keith. "I merely thought a demonstration would – "

"What's wrong with his heart?" asked Paul.

I felt the tiniest of hairs across the back of my neck.

"He can slow it to the pace of a hibernating bear's," answered Keith. "Right?"

He beamed.

"Keith," said Clare. "This isn't the place – "

"No," I answered. "It's fine. It's a fine place for parlor games and the like."

I glanced at Dr. Bashiri and noticed a trace of puzzlement.

I felt betrayed. Clare had shared something I hadn't exposed to anyone but her. And, in particular, she had apparently shared it with this guy, Keith. I wondered the context. *What else had she told him?*

About me? About us? And why?

My face was flushed with what I only imagined was a dark hue of crimson. When I focused back on the dinner guests circled around the living room, I realized the entire party was momentarily mute. They looked my direction.

"How about if you give me five minutes to relieve myself," I said, "and I'll come right back and Houdini you my torpor heart trick."

"Awesome!" said Keith, and I climbed the stairs toward Dr. Bashiri's second floor bathroom.

I splashed water on my face and stared at my reflection in the mirror. The low mumble of post dinner conversation was audible from the stairwell, and I had less desire than ever to return to the gathering, despite the hospitality of Clare's professor. Instead, I walked into the porcupine's room and sat. I fantasized an escape, images of Steve McQueen bouncing his motorbike over bumpy, barbed wired fields, the rear tire spitting gravel in a *fuck you all* spire.

I wondered if Clare wouldn't come find me and maybe explain why she had divulged my greatest secret with this guy Keith, what motivated that disclosure, and whether she'd apologize or calm my nerves or otherwise show, at least, she was still on my side. I don't know why it took me until that single, awkward moment to consider the question – *were we still on each other's sides? Was I on hers? Was she on mine? Weren't we supposed to, at the very least, be on the same side? What, or whom, were we permitting between?*

The more minutes that passed, and it took her at least fifteen to climb the stairs and find me, the more hopeless and astonished and lost I began to feel – rapidly accumulated worry and wonder.

"What are you doing?" Clare asked, her voice as hushed as she could manage under the circumstances. She spotted the open cage door and my crouch in the far corner of the alcove, pillowcase taut between my hands, no porcupine in sight.

"Close the door! The door!" I ordered, and Clare responded on reflex.

"What in the hell?" she asked.

"He ran into the closet."

Clare stared at me. Her eyes were swollen moons.

"I'm giving him five minutes to calm down," I said.

"How did he get out of his cage in the first place?" she asked. "And what are you doing with that pillowcase?'

"Clare, I watched this guy a good ten minutes. He's not walking a crooked pattern. No more than the rest of us."

"Will you answer me?"

"There's nothing wrong with this porcupine! He ought to be back out in the woods. Doing porcupine stuff."

"You can't kidnap Dr. Bashiri's porcupine," she whispered, her face red.

"It's not kidnapping, technically," I said.

"Technically?! Jesus, Jack."

"I was thinking we could slip him out, unnoticed, unchecked, and get him over to Krystoff for a second opinion. On the walking pattern. I mean, Krystoff's probably seen a thousand of these in the woods."

"A second opinion?"

"I could do it right now," I said. "I could bring him back before the dinner party is even over."

"Oh, that's a great idea!" said Clare. "I'll just tell everyone my boyfriend needs to step out a moment — with a bowling ball shaped, quill riddled pillowcase."

"There's got to be a side exit, somewhere. There almost always is."

"What?! No, Jack. The porcupine can't just not be here the next time he comes up the stairs. Don't you think that's something a person would notice?!"

"Okay," I said. "There may be a few wrinkles I need to iron out first..."

"Wrinkles?!"

"Well, come on," I said. "I'm not – I'm really *not* interested in heading back down those stairs just to show that whole room of people I barely know my heart experiment! Like it was some frat party gimmick. I mean, what in the hell?!"

"You don't have to," she said. "We can just forget that even happened."

"Forget it?! I mean really, Clare? You told people about that? Does everyone know about it?"

"Well, obviously, now," she said.

"Before now, I mean."

"Don't do this," she said. "Don't turn this around and make it my fault."

"Well, it's related," I said. "I mean, if we hadn't just had that scene downstairs, I really don't think we'd be standing in this room whispering about a god damned porcupine abduction scheme right now."

A clawed scurry from the closet broke our concentration.

"Oh, my god," hissed Clare.

"Let's get him out of there," I said. "Don't get too close to the tail."

"The tail?"

"They use it to launch their quills. We're lucky I've read up on this one."

Clare glared at me from across the room. "I'm getting Dr. Bashiri," she said.

"Wait, Clare."

"We'll tell him you got curious and accidentally let his porcupine out."

"And that's *not* fishy? Just give me some time to get him back into his cage. I can do this, really."

Clare folded her arms.

"I'll get him back in his cage," I said. "But I'm not climbing back down those stairs to show your friend Keith, and everyone else circled around that living room how I can turn my heart inside out."

Clare nodded.

"I'd rather just stay up here in this cage, with this porcupine, than have to do that...Ever."

Clare drew her shoulders back, and then released a quiet but lengthy sigh. She told me she was going to head back down to the party before others investigated. She told me she was relying on me to do the right thing.

"But I'm only waiting five minutes for you to do that," she said. "The right thing."

It wasn't, I suppose, the moment of solidarity I had hoped for, needed. And I wasn't willing to acknowledge how my own action, the porcupine liberation shenanigans, distracted the opportunity, hampered the desired outcome in the first place. I only focused, in that moment, on the separation I felt, from Clare, from that gathering, from the universe short of the woods.

And then, just like every other human tragedy that gulps its first breath as misguided inspiration and swiftly evolves into disaster through the seemingly benign sequential order of one small step marrying another and then the next, I soon found myself on the other side of Dr. Bashiri's alcove window, and then down the drain pipe to the first storey roofline, and then momentarily paused on the cold shingles of his back veranda before I knifed into the spired sea of juniper and yelped at the sharp pain that felt as though a bowie knife had sheared all the superior, inferior, flexor and extensor ligaments, muscles and tendons formerly cementing my ankle in place.

In hindsight, it probably wasn't the height that held primary responsibility for the injury as much as the extra twenty-four pounds of wriggling porcupine clutched in my fists.

Emulating the animal's own noted anomaly of mobility, it was now the human who initiated an angled walk across that dark lawn. I attempted to both cradle the pillowcase containing the balled animal and keep him clear of my own body, hoping, at this point, to steer clear of any additional damage to either one of us. Then I saw the crossing cones of flashlight approaching, the footsteps behind them wet punches into the sod.

For a moment, they seemed welcoming – the two oval beams of light. In between the throb of ankle pain, I imagined them two beautiful moons.

Maybe this is how the night sky appears through the eyes of a bear. The moon inhaled. Like standing in a sea foam tide, the galactic surge of starry water, the dewed smell of the moon's salt.

The flashlight orbs grew brighter, and I held perfectly still. The porcupine clicked its teeth. A pungent odor wafted through the pillowcase, and I pictured the two of us, man and porcupine, living out our remaining days in the clipped shadows of trees of the Scapegoat. I would pare the inner bark of fir trees, skin tufts of cellulose and help him out with the more difficult tasks of porcupine diet in a gesture of friendship and love.

For a brief moment, I honestly believed, or simply hoped, my future, both our futures, could become that easy.

Instead, there was only the cadence of my own breathing. I closed my eyes and waited for my heart to slow. It came easily. On reflex. I drew deep breaths, felt nothing but the soft chant of blood, a withered river, the gentle drumming in my ears a receding wave — farther and farther out to sea. I pressed my fingers against the flesh beneath my jaw and felt the weakening oscillation, until single, elongated pulses separated an expanding breadth of time. Until I could no longer feel a single thing. And then, my body drifted over the impossible river beneath me, up into the chalk of sky where my eyes adjusted with the nocturne vision of bears, the whole tangle of stars wrapped around my head.

My fingers opened toward them.

I was a thousand miles above the curve of woods and water, a thousand miles above the six individuals who collectively cradled the unharmed but seriously pissed off and pillowcased porcupine, and then checked the pulse and the shallow breath of the supine man on the dark sod who, moments before, sat across from them on a living room floor.

As I slowly, assuredly, drifted back to earth, my heart flooded in wonder about how much longer Clare could possibly continue to love me.

part three

I think it would be well, and proper, and obedient, and pure, to grasp your one necessity and not let it go, to dangle from it limp wherever it takes you. Then even death, where you're going no matter how you live, cannot you part. Seize it and let it seize you up aloft even, till your eyes burn out and drop; let your musky flesh fall off in shreds, and let your very bones unhinge and scatter, loosened over fields, over fields and woods, lightly, thoughtless, from any height at all, from as high as eagles.

Annie Dillard, Living Like Weasels

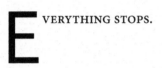

E VERYTHING STOPS.

Every…

possible...

thing.

You don't feel. A tremor billows beneath the bones of your chest – the force of a hummingbird's wings – but everything else is silent, still. You can sense the whir of the world beyond you, outside of you – others' voices, vehicles passing, the white noise of the universe's sonorous drone. But you are transported beyond it, outside of it. Your entire being hovers in wonder.

For that brief moment, before you process the loss, nothing hurts. The sensation is larger than pain. There is only awe.

And then you descend, slowly, unusually, back to where your body awaits your return. It greets you as an old friend, welcoming, wanting. And your chest feels as though it is filling with seawater. You wonder if you remember how to breathe. That's when the sensation transitions from numbness to hurt – the magnitude of loss that drowns you.

I had been through all this before. With Ben. And now, with Clare, the same awful wall of water was racing toward shore.

The sunlight pressed into the leaning oaks in our front yard and shaped long shadows across the sod, dark shapes resembling the curved fingers of giants. I moved quickly through them, with only the slightest tinge of pain from the twisted ankle earned during the thwarted porcupine liberation effort six weeks previous. I paused at the front door, spotted Clare through the window, her silhouette in a sea of half-filled cardboard boxes strewn across the living room. She turned toward me, and I moved through the doorway. Her arms were draped at her sides, and her eyes were wet. She attempted to smile a hello.

For a moment, I imagined how happy I would have been to see her if she hadn't been packing her things to leave.

"I'm really sorry, Jack," she said. She wiped tears from her cheeks. "I don't want this to be hard. And I don't even know – Jesus Christ," her voice caught, "I don't immediately know where I want this to lead, but…" She righted herself, inhaled a long breath, her eyes steady, brave. "I'm so sorry, Jack."

I stood, silent, in helpless wonder over what possible words I could string together in response. I set my backpack on the floor and came up with only two: "Don't go." Against Clare's silent response, I repeated them a number of times, as if they might eventually find a warm welcome, as if they might make a difference.

"It doesn't mean it will be permanent," she said, and wiped new tears. "But, I do need to do this. I need to do this, at least for right now."

I thought of the first night I held Clare in my arms. Her skin was the warmest, softest my lips had ever pressed against, and I simply breathed, my eyes locked into hers. Never in my life did I feel so fortunate to have fingers, eyes, lungs. An entirely new universe eclipsed the one that formally held in its place, gradients of gray replaced by luminiferous ether, particles replaced by waves.

Faced with the possibility of that beautiful world now disappearing, whisked permanently away, my heart felt blown as open and helpless as dandelion snow. *How is this happening?*

Clare and I had a long, drawn out argument the morning before she packed boxes, before I left the apartment in a huff. We had argued over the job at the ROTC gym – the job I lost due to spending too many weekends in the Scapegoat. During that conflict, I sensed Clare's fatigue. She seemed more worn, less alive, during the fight. I never imagined, though, she was near to packing her things to leave. I felt astonished, lost.

"It's not the fighting," she said. "It's not that – the stupid disagreements I know we could both work through if we wanted to, if we were more patient."

Her eyes were red, tired.

"It's all the sadness. And the distance, you know, between us. It seems endless."

I winced, bowed my head.

"I know you miss Ben," she said. "I know that. And you have

every right to go on missing him and remaining as sad as long as that missing lasts. Only..."

She waited and gathered her words.

"It seems like we're both drowning in it. The waiting. I think one of us has to find the strength to finally move past it."

I watched her from across the room. My heart descended further, like a sounding weight dropped into the Mariana Trench of the ocean.

"The thing is," she said. "I never noticed all my own sadness in this. All this time, I've only been noticing yours. It's like we've both been pulled under some tide that's been holding us under water or something. And for the longest time. And *you*, you sank all the way to the bottom – submerged completely. But I sank, too. Because it was inches instead of fathoms, or whatever, I believed my sinking, my drowning mattered less than yours."

I pictured Clare's white body drifting above me, her skin hued by seawater.

"It does matter less than yours, Jack," she continued, her voice even softer now. "I didn't lose a brother. But, mine still matters. For the longest time, I think I forgot that. Or ignored it. And I need – I'm pretty sure I need to fix that part of myself, you know?" Tears fell down her cheeks, and with the heel of her hand, she wiped them away.

"But I'm not drowning anymore," I said. "Don't leave right when I've finally found my way back to the surface."

"You haven't yet."

I watched her and waited.

"You're still so silent," she said. "Still retreating into the woods, still rooting through every new opportunity to lose yourself or turn our world on its ear."

I wanted more than anything to tell her of the warming place in my heart where I felt the broadened expanse of hope. Before this moment, the stronger force was hope.

"And I really don't think it matters so much at this point," she said. "I got here, found my way to standing on my own two feet. I'm figuring out how that feels. And I need to ask you to let me."

"Clare," I said. I curled my fingers into fists on my knees. "Give us a chance to – "

"Please don't, Jack," she said. "I've been thinking of this for the longest time. I've thought it forwards, backwards, side to side, and it's nearly impossible in every direction, but please, don't."

I contemplated the many times over the past few months Clare had approached the subject of separation and how, each time, I made sure the topic disappeared as swiftly as it had opened its wings. Each time, the thought of losing another important person in my life, of losing Clare, flooded me with panic. I don't think I bothered to consider, not until Clare so boldly announced it – it wasn't simply the space between us, pulling her away. There was also a separate need, one our relationship impacted but didn't embody, one I hadn't bothered to consider: Clare's independence.

We sat mute, my head bowed. Clare gazed through the window. And then she wordlessly turned back to her boxes, folded in the corners of those that had already been filled and quietly set new items in the rest. She moved the sealed boxes, one by one, out the door and into her black and gray Renault.

"We're just people," she said, before she left. "People do these things – they wander from one another. They explore new things, and if they're meant to be together, if their hearts matter in it enough, they find their way back."

"Or they don't," I answered.

For the longest while, after Clare hugged me goodbye, her whole body shivering, and after she walked out the door, hesitated, and then walked the sidewalk to her car, I remained still, as though everything that preceded that moment was illusion, as though the door would once again open, and Clare would step back through its opening. I waited for the last fragment of light to evaporate from the corner of the ceiling to give that hope every possible chance.

I thought only of Clare's pronouncement of *we're just people* and broke it into a muttered chant, as if there might be comfort there, as if it held a fragment of safety for the two of us, as if it was a credible prayer for salvation. And as if, from whatever exact geographic coordinate Clare had relocated herself, she was chanting it, too.

For the first several days following Clare's departure, I reconstructed, moment by moment, the history of our love. Each blurred image from our past became a new gem fished from a winding stream, a shining jewel turned in my fingers under moonlight.

If not in control of Clare's leaving, I hoped, at least, to shape what order I could across the sequence of events leading up to it.

Had Ben not skidded across the ice glazed Wisconsin interstate – had he made it home alive as he had every time that came before, had I not succumbed to resolute sadness, had my sleep not been mired by endless throngs of moon breathing bears, had I not secluded myself through whole successive seasons in a cube-shaped storage unit at the edge of Clear Lake in Minnesota, had I not fallen in love with the physics of torpor, had I not wandered all the way to the Scapegoat Wilderness of western Montana to collect, one by one, the amber follicles of grizzly bear hair, had I not balled up Clare's professor's pet porcupine into a pillow case and jumped from his upstairs window into his backyard in between the third course and dessert with said pillow case firmly clasped in my raised fist — had this entire series of tangentially related events not evolved, would any of the previous history that had shaped our love been salvageable?

In the open space following Clare's leaving, it was impossible not to realize I had left her first. I hadn't acknowledged it until then, not until I strung all the pieces together into one long ticker tape. My departure happened not in a single fell swoop, but over months of accumulated sleeping and waking moments and immeasurable degrees of silent separation. It happened during consecutive seasons of distraction. And carelessness.

I was the one who had wandered away, the one who dove the coldest layer of sea.

On the third day, I found strength to leave the apartment. I walked through the neighborhood, initially one circled block and then wider and longer zodiac patterns down sidewalks and alleys. I passed and re-passed the same slope-roofed houses and boxy garages in different angles of sun, the same dogs stretched lazily across separate slices of yard.

Sometimes I stood and watched their chests expand and contract.

Sunlight dappled through canopies of elm banking boulevard corners. It shifted shadow and light. People walked and biked by me, mute, my world a silent movie flickering over a screen, my heart a bird above the rushes, hovering.

I paused outside a yard where a child's blue plastic wading pool had been left since the final days of summer. A red plastic ball was held in place in the sheath of ice stretched across the pool's surface. I walked into the yard, moved close to the pool. The late winter sun had melted a layer of water beneath the ice. Probably this poor little wading pool had experienced perpetual freezing and thawing ever since August. Left unattended, the pool's water evaporated and then refilled with snow and then melt and then freeze and all over again, its water now cloudy, the plastic ball softly dented.

I thrust my feet through the pool's ice and felt the cold water suck at my ankles, soak through the canvas of my shoes and chill my toes. I stood motionless, my feet locked in the slush of the child's wading pool. I stared up through the crossing branches of elm. Willowy sunlight warmed my face. I smiled dumbly through the impossible revelation, these twenty-seven months past Ben's death,

I had successfully and resoundingly managed to free myself from the very thing that mattered and held my heart in place. If I had wanted to experience my heart and life liberated from every meaningful thing, save oxygen and gravity, every tangible force that formerly held them in place — if I had wanted to experience the helplessness of Ben's trajectory through sky, I could now score that mission a conditional victory.

I strung together the thirty-one days of March with a simple structure of repeated patterns, each day a near replica of the one that fell before it and the one that would follow.

Three times a day, I rose from my bed and warmed milk and boiled water. I emptied a single envelope of oatmeal (two envelopes mid-day and in the early evening) into a bowl. I poured the boiling water into the bowl, stirred it with a spoon. My face basked in the bowl's steam.

I poured warmed milk into a mug, swirled in a pinch of cinnamon. My kitchen window fogged, and I became momentarily mesmerized by the gentle effort of stirring sugar and cinnamon into the frothy milk. The creamy taste of this meal calmed me, filled me, again, with the desire to sleep.

Every night at dusk, I walked twenty-seven blocks across my neighborhood in the trajectory of the moon. I memorized each name stenciled across each mailbox; I memorized the colors of window trim, each style of door. I convinced myself if by some large, unexpected miracle of explosion our entire neighborhood was lost, pummeled into a dust of concrete, I alone could reconstruct it from simple memory, street by street, house by house, detailed in exact photographic clarity.

I heard from Clare only twice in the thirty-one days of March, two short notes left on my windshield. Collectively, her words to me numbered twenty-two. I counted them. I counted the consonants and vowels (107). I read them over and over. Together and separately, they failed to bring comfort, those 107 alphabetic bodies, even a moment's rest from the football field of ambiguity surrounding me.

One wind gust, and I could have fallen all the way to the moon.

Outside the Science Complex, the campus soil was soupy from the rain, and students stepped through slushy puddles in rubber boots and tennis shoes and cut angled patterns into mud across the seeping lawn.

Several hours passed before I spotted Clare moving down the steps, in conversation with two other students. Her arms clutched a stack of texts, a backpack slung over her shoulder.

Her long brunette hair flowed in the wind.

When her conversation broke, she walked to the bike rack, unlocked her bike, and rode through the campus. I ran behind her as fast as I could. Fortunately, she stopped at the edge of campus, on Arthur Street, and leaned the bike against a tree while she adjusted the cuffs of her jeans, tucked them into her socks. The delay allowed me to gain much of the distance between us.

She mounted her bike and rode down McLeod Avenue. She rode four blocks and turned right. My heart pounded a firm fist into my chest as she turned the corner and disappeared.

I slowed my run and leaned one arm against an oak for support. My lungs ached. I caught my breath and walked the four blocks to the street where I thought Clare had turned. I walked the neighborhood, eyed the rooming houses and apartment duplexes, searched for signs of her through the dark windows. *What curtains would she hang across her kitchen window? What posters would she tack against her living room wall?* I felt as though I was searching for the address of a long lost relative by mere intuition. Seven blocks down, luck turned my way. I spotted what looked to be Clare's bike chained to a tree. I found her last name inked across a fourplex doorbell directory, stared at the letters of her name, and the familiar shapes of her cursive lettering sped my heart.

"Had I known you were stalking, I would have baked a cake," she said, and parted the apartment door, a blue bandanna newly tied around her hair, her cheeks still flushed from biking.

I told her I had watched her bike by and wanted to say hello.

"I'd invite you in," she said. "But it doesn't feel like the right thing right now. I'm not ready to show you my new life."

I wondered what new life she could have germinated from the fracture of our separation, a handful of weeks along. *What did this new life entail? How far had it gone?* I wondered, too, all the reasons I had lost my place of welcomed entrance.

"Sounds so strange," I said. "New lives and waiting lists for viewing."

"You've lost weight, Jack," she said, her voice a little quiet. I could tell she was readying herself against any slip of emotion. I could tell it mattered to her that she didn't.

"Simple atrophy," I said. "Nothing that can't be healed by spring."

I missed every last part of her.

"This whole separation thing," I said. "I'm just wondering how far it goes."

"I wish there was an easier way," she answered, "but there isn't right now." And then she was silent, not giving me more than that.

"But we're not even talking," I said. "About anything."

"I can't yet," she answered. "I'm just...trying to be, I guess."

"Okay," I said. "Well, I want you to be. I just wanted to say hi."

Clare nodded.

"And to tell you I miss you," I added.

"I miss you too," she answered, tearing slightly.

"You do?"

"But that's separate," she said. "Missing you, right now, is separate from…everything else I need to focus on."

I nodded.

"Take care of yourself, Jack," she said softly before she turned, before she gently shut the door and disappeared behind its frame.

Without rolled newspapers sacked in a sling over my shoulder, it took forty-seven minutes to walk a nineteen-block perimeter of my neighborhood. It was the same route I walked in the cold blood of early morning, when I tossed the *Missoulian* across frozen lawns, when I crossed Dearborn, Livingston, South, Sussex, Central, Kent, then right on North before I crossed Thames to Lester and then back. I timed it repeatedly throughout the day, wore it into the concrete like rain against limestone.

I returned from each walk, steeped tea, waited a half hour, wondered what to do next to fill time, and then opened the front door with my knee, moved to the front stoop, looked into the roil of clouds along the spread of Mount Sentinel and walked again.

It was a runaway dog that motivated my one and only deviation from the rehearsed pattern, the aberration of routine that led to meeting Sumi. I was walking westward on Dearborn, toward my apartment, when I spotted the dog, a willowy Irish setter. It ran full gait down the asphalt, and its purple leash trailed behind. The dog wove in and out of traffic, a series of cars locking brakes to avoid colliding with the jaunting animal. I looked over my shoulder, saw no one in pursuit, turned on my heels and began chase. The dog had a good two, two and a half blocks on me, and was adding to the distance when we both got lucky and the dog became sidetracked by the smells embedded within a cluster of mailbox posts. It stopped, thrust its snout between the posts, circled the cluster and lifted its leg. By the time it had loped across the street toward a similar mailbox cluster, I had gained two blocks and walked the third. I didn't want my approach to startle the animal into a new relay.

The wayward Irish setter leapt across the curb when I approached, turned up an alley with a half-hearted trot, and then got lost in the sea of trashcans lined along the sides. It was enough of an opening for me to quietly slip behind the trailing leash and grasp its looped end.

The setter wagged its flared tail vigorously when I patted his flank. He pushed his snout into the crook of my neck, his tongue extended a half-foot from the exertion of the run, his breath warm and wet.

"Okay, boy…okay," I patted his side in reassurance as I double-wrapped the leash around my wrist.

We traced our steps in reverse, both of us winded from the run, and we gradually gained back our breath. The dog continued to lurch toward the street in terse pulls of leash, but I managed to keep him mostly from the curb.

We walked up and down Dearborn, then Livingston, then South, a good twenty minutes, before I spotted her, a young woman wearing a 1950s honeysuckle pink crown hat, velvet ribbon tied in a bow on one side. She hurried down the sidewalk, a pair of books wedged beneath her arm as she moved toward us.

I smiled, relieved, reassured this was the woman we were looking for, dog and I. We waited as she approached. The setter lurched for her when she got close.

"I am so sorry…oh, Charlie…so, so sorry."

"He's okay."

Her forehead was speckled with perspiration, her eyes welled. It was clear her relief and fear were still intertwined.

"There was a squirrel – I had all these books. He made a lunge and then – "

"It's okay. It's okay," I said. "He's fine. Was sniffing up a huddle of trashcans when I caught up to him. I'm happy we found you, though.

No dog tag."

"I know. I know. He has one, I just – "

"It's okay. Here," I said, and handed her Charlie's leash.

I noticed the ring around her third finger as I let go of the leash, a thin band and sliver of diamond. She seemed so young to be married, a freshman or sophomore at the University, I supposed. Her hands were tiny.

"Thank you. I really – he's an enthusiastic guy, but this is the first time he's broken away like that."

"Every dog has his squirrel moment," I said.

She responded with a short burst of laughter and then wiped her free hand beneath her nose. She sighed.

"You okay?" I asked.

"Yep. I dropped a bunch of books somewhere back there, though." She looked back over her shoulder. "Should try to find them."

I glanced at the two she was holding. Salinger's *Franny and Zooey* and Joyce's *Portrait of an Artist*.

"One of my favorites," I said. I gestured to her books, smiled, and turned to walk away.

"Which one?" she asked. "Hey! You know – I've seen you on our block."

I turned.

"You walk by, like...all the time."

I felt my face flush.

"I've counted," she said. "Seven times one day."

"Then you missed at least another seven passes," I answered. "Usually it's about a dozen total. Or twenty."

"You must like walking," she said.

"It's something I do, lately," I said, and wondered which house or apartment along my route could be hers. If she waited, I could have described each building in linear order until describing hers.

"Do you – are you a student here, too?"

"Paperboy," I said, and she smiled at me and appeared to wonder how to take my response.

I wanted to leave it at that, the duration of our meeting. I was more than ready to retreat to my silent apartment. But there was something about her that disarmed me. The honeysuckle pink crown hat probably played a part.

We spent the next twenty minutes in each other's company. We walked east on South and stopped intermittently to pick up another of her discarded books, each one haphazardly fanned across the concrete, each one another tome of classic literature: Rilke, another Salinger (*Nine Stories*), Wallace Stevens, a cover-worn Plath. When we got to the final one, she was hoisting a stack of seven, making me wonder how she had ever conceived of handling all seven and bounding Irish setter at once.

Forty-seven days had passed since hearing from Clare, since our conversation in the doorway of her apartment. Sometimes, I counted and recounted the number of days across my kitchen calendar, fresh ink dots marking each day. My heart sank at each total.

My feelings towards her, my missing her, were frayed beyond the coherence required for succinct love letters. Nor were missives of *any* content probably welcomed, at the moment. Instead, I spent two entire days cutting paper elephants with thoughts of stringing the herd from my heart to hers.

It began with a stack of heavy rag paper. I stenciled a rounded elephant shape, detailed its eyes, the folds of its ears and curved trunk with tiny dots of ink. I took care in cutting the shape, the width of my open hand, from the paper.

I set the first newly cut elephant against the floor. It was beautiful; its elongated trunk hovered above its feet. I stared at it twenty minutes before I leaned in and inked a new elephant shape and cut it free from the paper.

By the end of the two-day marathon, I had sixty-four paper elephants, trunk to tail, stretched across my floor – from bedroom wall, across the living room, all the way to the front door. Some sat on their rear, some leaned into the earth on bended knee, some balanced on two legs and hoofed the sky; some stretched their trunks taut.

A rat's nest of sheared rag paper shrapnel was mounded next to my desk, tufts of shavings scattered through the living room.

I collected the paper pachyderms one by one, pressed them into a box, sealed them shut, and without much thought, inked Clare's new address and dropped them at the post office, my own private herd of paper elephants cast adrift into the world, in search of water, in search of Clare.

Six days after I rescued her dog, I ran into Sumi for the second time. I was on my fifth walk of the day when she waved at me from her front porch. She sipped from a steaming mug clasped between her mittened hands.

Charlie, his tail wagging, greeted me at the gate.

"I thought you might live here," I said. "I thought I recognized Charlie."

The house she lived in was small – a converted garage. Charlie had a tiny fenced yard all to himself. I imagined he spent much of his day lounging in the yard sun.

"Well…" I said at the first pause. "Nice seeing you again."

"Why is it you walk this neighborhood so many times a day?" she asked. "Did you lose a set of car keys?"

"Something like that," I answered. I thought of the polar bear trapped in the Como Park Zoo in Saint Paul, how he'd pace back and forth on the same trajectory in his pen, how his paws, over time, wore a circular imprint into the concrete. Maybe I was becoming the caged polar bear of Missoula, the neighbors watching my stereotypic movement disorder from the other side of the bars. Or Sumi was.

"Will you do me a favor?" asked Sumi.

"Maybe."

"Take Charlie for a walk?"

"Now?"

"On one of your seventeen passes through the neighborhood," she answered. "I don't think he gets the exercise he needs from me or my husband. And as long as you're walking anyway..."

Charlie had retreated to the corner of the lawn, his eyelids black crescent moons, his wide head angled across his legs. He basked in the sun. The idea of walking companionship, however mute, immediately appealed to me.

"I don't know if you should let a complete stranger walk your dog."

"It's okay," she said. "I trust you. You already saved him once from running to Frenchtown."

"Maybe."

"His leash is hanging right here." She lifted it from the nail on the deck. "Clip it on him and away you go."

She had the warmest smile.

"And don't forget to bring him back," she said.

Sixty-four paper elephants, unexplained, posted via the U.S. Postal Service, solicit no response from estranged girlfriends. That's what I learned. I waited a week, but no word.

In response, I opted to up my game. I drove to the Missoula Craft and Hobby Emporium and wandered the shelves: blue eyed doll heads, bodiless, and staring serenely ahead, sweater patterns and zippers, lamp shade kits, colorful beads and fake flower garlands. There were aisles of materials to choose from. Twenty minutes later, I walked out of the store with a twenty-pound block of paraffin wax, a jar of cranberry scent, boxed dye tablets, a spool of wick, and, the critical piece, a monkey shaped candle mold.

I had a new plan.

The next time I passed Sumi's house, I paused at the gate. Charlie was splayed across the front deck. His paws drooped over the deck's edge. I unclipped the fence door and walked toward him; his tail swept across the decking.

I saw no sign of Sumi or her husband. I yanked the leash from its nail, clipped it onto Charlie's collar, muttered one "let's go, boy," and he bounded through the open gateway, my body trailing behind him.

It took me a number of blocks before I was able to even our stride. Left to his own momentum, Charlie would streak through the neighborhood with staccato stops at nearly every tree or signpost. The first few blocks, my arm was yanked from its socket in nearly every direction. But, I soon learned the trick of short, sharp pulls at his leash to bring him in closer and set our rhythm.

The sun on our shoulders, my heart drummed from our accelerated pace, and it felt good to be walking through the neighborhood with Charlie. For the first time in weeks, I felt the renewed energy, the relational surge of spirit that comes from forward movement, regardless of its relative accomplishment. For the first time in weeks, something other than the absence of Clare was keeping me company, forcing a forward trajectory.

Sometimes I walked Charlie six or seven times a day.

• • • • •

I became so attached to Charlie during my walks through the neighborhood, if I passed Sumi's house and didn't see him in the yard, I felt a pang of absence.

On one such pass, I came across Charlie three blocks up, walking alongside Sumi.

"This is good," said Sumi. "I've been wanting to join you on one of these. Beginning to get jealous of Charlie getting to know you so well."

"There's not much to know. A guy doing a lot of walking. Sometimes with a borrowed dog."

"He's in much better shape, thanks to you," she said.

"We both are."

I joined Sumi and Charlie on their stroll. I refrained from steering their direction. I decided it was bad manners, although I (and seemingly Charlie, too) took note at every turn Sumi took that deviated from our normal pattern. Our pace was also slowed in stride with hers.

When Sumi asked me what brought me to Montana, I merely answered "Bears," surprised only slightly by my immediate candor.

"Bears?"

"Mostly I dreamt them. Anywhere from one to thirty nightly. Here, I get the opportunity to count them for real."

"How's that?"

"In the Scapegoat. Last summer and this," I answered. "It's a part of a research project by a professor at the University."

"Your dreams are part of a study, or the bears are?" she asked.

"I don't know," I said. "Maybe both."

When I asked Sumi what brought her to Montana, she said her excuse was not nearly as enigmatic as mine.

"I came here in the middle of my sophomore year from Oregon

State," she said. "One year ago. I needed a change. For a bunch of reasons. My brother was here. I love the mountains. So I packed up my Civic and drove east. It didn't take much effort to transfer the credits."

She sipped purple juice through a straw-punctured box.

"You were married when you moved here?" I asked.

"No, no, no, no, no..." she said. "That wasn't a possibility then. To my husband."

"No?"

"I hadn't met him yet. He's a friend of my brother's. I got here – we met...if it wore a t-shirt, it would have the word 'rebound' written all over it."

"But you married?"

"Three months after we met," she said. "Impulse control – not my strong suit."

"It's none of my – "

"I don't mind," she said. "Really, I'd rather talk about it with somebody. It could probably help."

"And Charlie?" I asked.

"Charlie moved with me from Oregon. I've had him since he was a puppy." She patted his flank. "He's my savior. I keep a box of tennis balls he's gummed away to nothing. There's probably fifty of them. I can't, won't, part with a single one."

We walked across Bancroft, and Sumi leaned into Charlie's scruff and unclipped his leash.

"He should be okay here," she said, and Charlie bounded across the Sentinel High School football field. "The day you rescued him from his joy run was an anomaly. Normally he minds me."

We watched him bolt alongside the running track. When Sumi whistled, he slowed.

"And you?" Sumi asked.

"Me?"

"Marriages? Divorces?"

"Somewhere…in the middle," I answered.

Sumi looked at me.

"We moved here together," I said. "My girlfriend. Or I guess I moved here and she followed."

"And?"

"We're still here. Both of us. We're just not together, exactly. I haven't heard from her in a while."

"What's that about?"

"She's doing her own thing right now, I guess." I didn't know how to answer her better.

"And you?" she asked. "Are you waiting for her while she does her own thing? Counting bears and the days apart?"

"I'm trying not to," I said. "But the truth is, I think I'm waiting with every breath — each swimming cell in my body. I am…one whole monument to waiting."

Sumi smiled. She nodded. "That bad," she said.

In early April, the tongue of spring was licking the napes of our necks. Snow patches hunkered stoically in the low divots across lawns, a daily, sometimes hourly, retreat. Trees, empty but for small stubs of shriveled leaves on their lower limbs, were dotted with new buds, tiny bursts of greens and maroon.

I spent the first several days of that same thaw oblivious to it. In my improvised kitchen laboratory, I hammered a screwdriver into a wax slab. Shards shot across my kitchen counter, and I pooled the clods and fragments into a pan set over a low stove burner and watched the wax slide into melt. My entire apartment steeped in the aroma of melted paraffin.

I dropped dark blots of red dye, crimson swirls that corkscrewed like question marks as they merged into the molten wax. I squeezed a few drops of cranberry scent into the vat and stirred. I lifted the pan over the upside-down monkey mold and poured a long drizzle of wax into its belly. I pulled the wick taut through the center of the form, looped its end around a pencil, and set it across the mold opening.

After an hour cooling, I held the monkey embryo in my hands, the little upside down chimp's protruding abdomen against my fingers. He felt warm, alive. I could have held him forever.

The next morning, I woke early and eagerly approached the monkey mold, now solid and room temperature. I spread the edges of the mold apart carefully and removed one nearly perfect and whole candle monkey. I drew a razor blade over the excess wax seam line, and a long shaving of red wax curled and reached for the floor. I trimmed the wick on both ends.

I turned my monkey candle in my hands and wondered if this was how gods felt when they kissed new, beautiful life forms through the dry dust of stars. With his squat shape, knees bent and long-toed feet pointed up into his belly, he was the most perfect thing I had created.

For the first time in many days, I smiled stupidly through the bay window into the empty trees. My heart thumped.

I spent the next ten successive days chipping paraffin, melting wax, dropping dye tablets, pouring the mix into the monkey mold and waiting a full night before carefully removing a new form.

Days later, I had lined a neat row of eleven monkey candles around the perimeter of my kitchen, each one a slightly different color, each one glimmering in the incandescence of the overhead kitchen light.

Who else would do this? I stared at my creations with complete self-satisfaction.

Too excited to keep my enthusiasm for my wax monkey battalion all to myself, on the next run to the craft emporium for more paraffin, I drove toward Sumi's house, and slowed my truck by her fence line. Charlie raised his head from the lawn, his ears perked.

It was a Tuesday morning, late enough for Sumi's husband to be off at the auto parts store where he worked, so I left my pickup idling and knocked on her door.

"You've got to see what I've been working on the last several days," I told her when she opened the door, her hair wrapped in a green and blue swirling scarf. She held a worn book of Dick Hugo poems, wedged open with her thumb.

"Okee dokey," she said.

Sumi rode with me back to my apartment. She eyed the large slab of paraffin neatly wrapped in brown paper and wedged between us in the front seat of the truck.

When we came through the door of my apartment, she immediately spotted the collection of monkey candles. They were hard to miss, lined up along the counter, each one a different color.

"I've got four more to make," I told her. She stared quietly at each one.

"Monkey candles?"

"Not just monkey candles," I told her. "Monkeynaut candles."

"Monkey…nauts," she said.

"Replicas, anyway," I said.

"What's a monkeynaut?" she asked.

"Long before NASA had the guts to send humans up into orbit, they sent a series of monkeys and chimpanzees into the sky."

"They did," said Sumi. She plucked a purple wax monkey from the counter top.

"That one is Gordo," I told her. "He was a squirrel monkey, shipped off in the nose cone of a rocket in 1956. Gordo survived the flight but drowned in the Atlantic when the nose cone flotation device turned out to be crap."

Sumi turned back to the collection.

"Those next two," I told her, "are Able and Baker. They both survived a three-hundred-mile sub-orbit, but Able died four days after. Trouble with anesthesia from a post-flight surgery to remove a monitoring device."

"Monkeynauting is dangerous business," answered Sumi.

"You have no idea," I said. "The first several monkeynauts were pretty much pummeled into dust at impact, one after the other. I mean, the whole shooting match was fucked up shit."

I thought of telling Sumi about the bear cubs the U.S. military drugged and strapped into the ejector seats of the first supersonic bomber planes – how the helpless cubs were propelled into sky the speed of sound in their army green test capsules, and how they fell to earth with shattered bear bones, but I couldn't bring myself to even talk about that injustice.

"Yorick," I told her, "was the first monkeynaut to live through an actual space flight. And I don't think that was until – early fifties. Even the later monkeynauts, like Goliath and Bonnie?" I shook my head. "Not good." I told her how Goliath, a beautiful, one-pound squirrel monkey, was pounded into oblivion before the poor guy's capsule even left the ground. And about how Bonnie made a nine-day orbit, the end of the sixties, but then suffered a heart attack after she returned – the fatal blow blamed on severe dehydration.

"The monkeynaut union better get their asses all over this," Sumi muttered. She set the Gordo candle down on the counter and turned to me. Her expression reflected concern.

"I know. They're not perfect," I said. "I only had one wax mold. A chimpanzee. And the actual monkeynauts ranged from rhesus, squirrel, Philippine, and pig-tailed monkeys. Only a few of the later ones were actually chimps."

"Still," said Sumi. "A loving tribute."

I smiled, nodded.

"Where is this leading?" asked Sumi. She smiled.

"I'm sending them to Clare."

She eyed me. "You are?"

"Not all at once. One at a time. The same order they were originally sent into space. Able and Baker will be shipped together, of course. And Patricia and Mike."

"You're sending your girlfriend – your separated girlfriend – successive wax monkeys in the mail?"

"God bless their souls."

"And this tells her – *what*?" she asked.

I paused. I thought of telling Sumi about the paper elephants that were sent *en masse* before the monkeys even took root as an idea, but then I wondered if taking Sumi back to my apartment was a good idea. I wondered if she wasn't beginning to think twice about our friendship. That, and I really had little explanation to better illuminate the concept behind my planned wax monkey orbits.

"Have you talked with Clare at all?" she asked.

"No," I answered. "Not for weeks."

"It's – the clarity of communication is a little…absent," she said. "A dozen roses, shipped in a box. *That* she'd likely get. Fifteen monkey candles shipped one or two at a time…What are you – "

"It's not as though I just want to tell her something…insignificant."

Sumi waited. We were both silent.

"I know," she said. "I know this."

"I mean," I said. "Just getting her to smile, again. That would be something, right?"

I wondered if the last two weeks I had spent molding wax monkeys wasn't a complete waste. I wondered why it took me until now to consider the possibility.

"This Clare," said Sumi. "Do you love her?"

"More than the world."

"And you miss her?"

"You have no idea."

"Okay," she said. "Then tell her that. Tell her those two simple things. If there's the right place to tell her."

Sumi leaned against my sofa and sat, crossed her legs. She tucked her hands into the pockets of her wool coat. I watched her eyes wander across my living room, taking in new information, assessing the damage. Her gaze moved from the mounds of paraffin wax shrapnel, to the journals and notebooks I had routinely filled and then nested one on top of the other, to the mountain of unwashed dishes piled in the sink. My entire apartment told the story of a man whose better heart was in limbo.

Sumi looked me in the eyes. She nodded.

"All of this hurts, Sumi," I told her, finding it easier to level with her than improvise a brave face. I cradled a red monkey candle, Ham, in my palm. "Every ounce of it. I miss Clare. I can't stop thinking about her. I can't stop myself from wishing there was something, one thing I could do to try to put things back together…to put *some*thing back together. And when the person you love stops believing in you – I mean, it's sort of impossible not to be devastated by that."

"That's true" she said. "It is sort of impossible not to be devastated by that."

"You've been there, haven't you?" I asked.

"Been where?"

"You know. In the place where – where the things you wanted

and the place you are…they couldn't be farther from one another."

"I can barely remember *not* being in that place," she answered. "Look – I can tell you miss her. I know you love her. Is there any way you can tell her and have her hear you? Is there any difference you can make – telling her exactly those words?"

"That's the thing," I said. "I feel like I've lost my right to say *any*thing. The last few years, I asked her for so much. I'm already way beyond the limits of the loan."

"Love isn't a loan," said Sumi.

"Maybe," I said. "But it can become one."

Sumi watched me. She bit her lower lip.

I told her: "I feel like a seven ounce squirrel monkey orbiting the stratosphere."

Most of the time, it was exactly like that – as though my body hurtled helplessly through space, and my elbows gently clocked the walls of my US Army-issued AM-13 rocket while the entire mission plunged through the earth's atmospheric blanket, and like Ham, Gordo, Bonnie and Goliath and all the others, I was just another reluctant volunteer strapped into the pilot seat of an autonomously powered missile that knifed the choppy saline of the Atlantic while spent peanut shells swam, confetti-like across the ceiling, and mounded a soft nest across my lap. I was the restrained witness, separated from the one I loved and forced to simply watch the red flower of sun fade across the center of the windshield – the distant star that ebbed within the liquid blur of salted water, and left me in trance-like wonder over whether or not the two of us: sun and me, Clare and me, would ever see each other again.

To love someone and lose her – it's one thing. But to love someone and have her leave you is another thing entirely. The first is an endless loss, the second an endless wound.

I was miserable without her. I woke in the cold stretches of night, paralyzed by an ache that spread its fingers, one by one, across my chest. When the room bathed in morning, I was staring at her empty side of the bed.

Clare was the softest place my life, the warmest place my body had known. I was clueless how I might survive her exit, be it permanent. But when I envisioned her returning, I felt as though I was pretending, hoping for something no longer anywhere close to mine.

Sumi and I drove north on I-90. The sky was dark; a pregnant half-moon leaned belly forward over the curve of mountains. It was Friday night. She told her husband she was out with friends from school. We got in my truck and drove, both of us feeling a momentary need to free ourselves from Missoula.

We drove through the scattering of nearby towns – Frenchtown, Huson, Alberton – silent towns with houses and storefronts with dark windows that reflected our headlights and the stars, bar doorways hued in neon.

For a while we listened to the sound of the wheels. They whirred over the pavement, and both of us were lost in the web of our own thoughts. I wondered if the evolving scene before us seemed as sad to Sumi as it did to me, each new town we came to more doleful than the one before it. Or, maybe it felt like sadness to be driving away from something we'd both need to return to, Sumi and I taking momentary reprieves from our separate, isolated worlds. When the evening ended, it would be a toss-up which of us was more alone.

"Your marriage?" I asked. "Was it always, I don't know, difficult? Like even from the start?"

"Oh, we're going *there* again?"

"I don't know, I just – "

"I suppose it's hard for you, your heart all balled into a wet rag.

You know, pining her."

"I'm not always," I said.

"You are always. Anyways – I don't know. If it was always difficult. Sometimes you fall for someone because they are standing right in front of you when you need someone to be. And you dress them up as the something you want them to be."

"Is that what happened?"

"Our imaginations," she said. "They get us in trouble." And then she reflected on that a moment and said: "On the other hand – lack of imagination in relationships – equally damaging."

I thought of telling Sumi how I had learned the trick of slowing my heart to single contractions of blood across whole minutes.

I pulled the truck off the interstate and coasted the side streets of Alberton until we stopped in a parking lot alongside a fried chicken store. We sat in the wash of the store's illuminated sign – a paper bucket bulging with breaded chicken drumsticks and thighs.

"Hungry?" I asked.

"Not me," she said. "But, this is good. Let's just sit here a while and watch what happens."

Sumi had dark bangs she often whisked with the back of her hand, bangs that flicked with the wind. She had dark brown, coffee eyes, full cheeks, and lips that looked as though they had been stung by bees: red, swollen, the kind of lips you never stop imagining kissing until you do, and even then, after.

We left the truck idling. The truck's heater purred, and I imagined how the sounds of this parking lot would transform over the coming weeks, the chirp of crickets, the drone of deep fat fryers through screened windows. We were weeks away from the erratic thaw into spring.

I wondered if it were true, as Sumi stated it, that she and her husband had never truly been in love, just in love with being in love, in wanting. I wondered if it was true they had wandered into each other's lives and arms as a means to get past the separate painful relationships that preceded their meeting. I couldn't imagine merging my life with someone I wasn't in love with. But thinking of it turned my thoughts to Clare, and I wanted desperately to be liberated from those thoughts. At least for a while.

"Well," I said. "I suppose we should head home and see what thrilling highlights we missed while we were away."

"Yeah," she said. "Because I'm pretty sure our lives are in exactly the same place we left them, and we wouldn't want to miss a minute of seeing them crumpled into their sad little corners."

I smiled, watched the stars try to poke their heads through the sky's haze.

"Have you ever stared up into a snowfall just to feel it blanket your body?" Sumi asked.

"I used to," I said. "Long time ago."

"I still do," she said. "Just to watch it descend. Light against my eyelashes. It blots the whole sky, a little at a time. And eventually it becomes part of you. It presses into your body, the collective weight of feathers – the universe descending a molecule at a time."

Sumi leaned toward the window. I watched her breath form against the glass. There were moments like this one I wanted to press my lips against hers, certain the sensation would be nothing more than the softness and warmth we both craved and missed, but sure, too, what followed would be a fall neither of us was in a position to handle.

I took a deep breath, felt it tighten across my chest.

We sat a while longer. We watched the slow shuffle of fried chicken patrons. They emerged from the store and walked to their cars or down the sidewalk. Each time the restaurant's door parted, steam swirled into the sky.

And then Sumi's hand folded gently into mine.

• • • • •

Three months had passed since hearing from Clare. More precisely, eighty-seven days; I rounded up.

The truth is, I didn't know what the current rules were for contact. I was trying to give her space, and hoped she'd remain connected. When she failed to keep in touch, I hoped the absence of me from her life would inspire renewed attachment. But three months in, I gave in to my own missing and took up Sumi's suggestion of the direct approach – I'd communicate from the heart. I wrote Clare a simple letter, re-read it several times to make sure it was right, and then I folded it twice, slipped it into an envelope, and penned Clare's name across the envelope's center.

There it was – my letter, my true feelings about our separation, about Clare, about my missing her and wanting to work through our differences, large, small and otherwise.

Based on my recent failure to win a response from my United States Postal Service-delivered paper elephant herd, I decided to bypass government assistance for this one and hand deliver the envelope, the letter – from my hands to Clare's.

But a baker's dozen of minutes later, when I stood outside her duplex, on the soft wood of the landing, envelope in hand, I realized the mode of delivery choice in this case was probably a mistake – another, in an ever lengthening line.

The view through Clare's front door window revealed an empty kitchen, scattered pots and pans – the aftermath of a prepared meal. Flickering candlelight from the living room basked the ceiling. These small signs of hidden life revealed stilled my heart.

She's hosting dinner parties? My life is three meals of oatmeal a day and a weekly change of sweatpants. A seventeen-block walk through the neighborhood on the half hour. And she's hosting parties?

Clare's social life was obviously her own business. I had no right to trespass or question. It was the angle of contrast between her life and mine – the obvious difference in emotional impact our floundering relationship had brought our two separate worlds that disarmed me. I knew it was there – but coming face to face with proof of it was jarring, a reflection of my own heart's centrifugal force.

And then that obtuse, warm muscle in the center of my chest wind sprinted across an open field. I spotted a man's Mackinaw coat sloped over the arm of an empty chair in the corner of Clare's kitchen. It was the only clear evidence I noticed of individual dinner guests.

I had trouble swallowing.

Instead of slipping my enveloped letter under her door, or tucking it into her mailbox, I clasped it in my hand and backed away from the landing all the way into the neighbor's dark lawn. My heart pounded. It leapt against my rib cage with the force and subtle nuance of a battering ram.

I told myself to take a deep breath, turn back to my truck, stick the keys in the ignition and drive directly back to my apartment, lock the doors, hide the car keys, swallow them if I had to, and wait for this missile launch of anxiety to wane. It was, perhaps, the sole benefit of repeatedly walking across the burning embers of panic: learning its anatomy – its excruciating, white heat launch, followed by the seemingly eternal and ambiguous main act that swamped the room and rolled like sea water toward the ceiling, and then the eventual, if you were patient enough, calm. Or forgetting.

Though it could take hours or days, a period of calm (or forgetting) would eventually surface. It was the one reward of episodic psychological impairment I continually reminded myself existed, if perpetually at arm's reach or farther.

Breathe in. Breathe out. Wait. Wait. Wait.

I backed up, leaned against the neighbor's maple. From my stance in that wet lawn, I couldn't see anything through Clare's living room windows but ceiling. But the lowest maple limb was less than a foot from my nose.

Branch by branch, I pulled myself past newly formed buds – little verdure hands clasped in prayer. In a matter of moments, the dewed grass was blurred yards beneath my feet. Swallows swooped beneath the telephone line strung across the backyards, and I peered past them into Clare's warmly lit living room.

Clare didn't notice me – her estranged boyfriend scaled halfway up her neighbor's backyard maple tree. She was too busy embracing a bushy haired man in the archway of her kitchen – or, more accurately, letting him embrace her. Her head was bowed. She was talking. The man had one arm slung around her waist, the other resting on her shoulder. His fingers caressed the back of her neck. They wreathed the soft tangles of her hair.

To her credit, Clare's body language indicated she wasn't at ease with the man's embrace, the intimate proximity of it. What this man missed, inches from his nose — Clare's reticence, I saw clearly a full address away. And that small but weighted realization provided me the emotion I recognized as hope.

My heart hammered through the maple's thin bark and its vascular cambium clear down to its muddy roots. I saw no signs of other dinner guests – just this thick-haired man with his arms around the woman I still loved. Then he pulled her into his chest, and I viewed, finally, his parched complexion – Keith Hollbeck, the older, dour-faced grad student acquaintance of Clare's whose preoccupation with the state of Clare's heart seemed, from my wholly subjective view, more heavily weighted with self-interest than altruism. Through the shock, my initial reaction was – *does it have to be this guy?*

Before we had separated, Clare revealed enough about her friendship with Keith, how he pressed her for details of our relationship, eagerly commiserated, and readily offered advice along with his shoulder. Not that it was impossible his support stemmed from a sincere place of platonic caring, free of conflict – just that from my vantage point, across the wind-swept field, the clouds of that possibility (and their fleet advance) pooled more than a trace of umber. But the storm I hadn't predicted, or prepared myself for, was the possibility Clare might be receptive.

I fell onto the lawn and stifled a yelp when my ankle twisted into the soil.

"Oh, for *fuck*," I wheezed and grabbed a clump of soil. I crawled several paces and then paused to catch my breath. The same ankle I twisted during my failed porcupine abduction throbbed anew.

I realized I still had the chance to make a clean escape. I could limp off to my truck and drive home, the entire episode unnoticed but by angels. But the angels, it appeared, were off duty. Not one of them restrained me from bounding up the concrete steps of Clare's duplex. None threw themselves in front of my clenched fist when I pounded it against the glass of her front door.

Silhouetted through the gauze curtain, Clare's body seemed to leap across the room toward the entrance. She parted the door, saw it was me, and immediately opened it wide.

"Jack!" she said, at a loss for breath.

"Can I come in?"

"What are you doing here?!" she asked.

"I'm really not sure."

Clare hesitated, her mouth open.

Keith's eyes darted from the two of us back toward the living room. If he was searching for a secret exit or trap door, none appeared. Instead of fleeing, he pulled a 180 and struck a casual pose – thrust his hands into his pockets, a stance more aligned with a man waiting for a bus at the corner or a sandwich from a microwave than one who, seconds before, wrapped those hands and their ten fingers around someone else's girlfriend, however estranged.

"I've got company," Clare said.

I nodded. "I see that."

"You remember Keith," she said.

Trapped into re-introductions, Keith made the sporting gesture of extending his hand and knit a scythe-shaped grin from ear to ear.

His hand, holding nothing, remained extended, and I neatly folded the chest of his T-shirt in my fists and walked him backwards into the farthest kitchen wall.

"Really?" I said. "You want to go from holding her to shaking my hand? It's that easy for you? Just like that?"

"You need to calm down," he said, in a tone straining to sound both calm and instructive. "We can talk about this."

"We can?" I asked.

"Jack," said Clare.

"No, I'd really like to find out what Keith here has to say. About the this we can talk about."

Keith paused, appeared to be coalescing his thoughts. And then, in a low monotone, he said: "We can talk, but maybe after you remove your talons from my chest."

"Talons?"

"Let go," said Clare.

The kitchen door swung open in a burst of wind.

"What does he mean by talons?"

"Jack."

"No, really. Do you get that part? Like an eagle?"

"Just let go, okay?"

"I would – I'm really struggling here with the whole talons thing. Who uses that word? In this context?"

Keith's expression remained stoic, even. He stared wordlessly back at me, unflinching, save from the one sign of storm he couldn't restrain from its determined liberation of his otherwise millpond demeanor – the carotid artery that jump-roped beneath the vellum of his neck with atrial fibrillation the fervor of Clayton "Peg Leg" Bates across an open stage.

I stared at that antic vein, calculated the surging heart rate beneath its zeal and assessed it some twelve times the rate of bear.

"Let go of him, Jack."

Clare's voice softened. She touched my shoulder, and I let go.

As soon as I did, the exact moment my fingers released the cotton of Keith's wrinkled T-shirt, I felt an immediate and resounding wave of wonder over the entire collection of successive actions that preceded that moment, as though I was viewing the tape delay of my own life, bewildered by the playback – each second that elapsed from the moment I bounded across that dark lawn, through the doorway and across the amber lit kitchen, each muscle and action soaring from adrenaline, void of reason, and the dark sea of surrendered frailty beneath them.

I took one step back, leaned an arm against Clare's kitchen counter, and waited for the rolling sea to diminish an inch, at least, from the umbra of the moon.

Where am I? What am I doing?

Searching for a mooring, I spotted my red sauté pan and iron clad pot across the room, near the sink – a momentary welcomed and familiar sight. And then I followed the drizzle of green sauce inked across the stove top and the tidy nest of chicken bones cleaned of meat. Based on that evidence and the pungent bouquet, I surmised the dinner Keith and Clare shared had been a chicken curry – one Clare wasn't versed in, and I could only assume Keith prepared on her behalf, helping himself to her kitchen, and my old pots and pans, just as he helped himself to deciding, moments before, ours was a situation we three could "talk about."

If my heart needed one final thwack against its gunwale to realize the depths of its predicament, the sight of that curry-mudded pot was it – the very item my brother Ben had given to me when I moved into my first apartment, and the last formal gift Ben would present me in his abbreviated lifetime.

There it was.

My eyes welled, and I wanted to move immediately across that kitchen floor, pull that pot into my hands, place it directly beneath the faucet, and wash every last trace of curry and recent history from its being, erase it from its memory, and wrap the item in my arms. The only thing stopping me from pursuing exactly those actions was the realization I would be unable to accomplish them without breaking down – maybe completely. And I wasn't going to let that happen with Keith bearing witness.

You've taken enough. You don't get that, too.

Instead, I stared at that pot, across the room, and the oblong splatters across the stove – the vain imprint of a murder victim stumbling homeward, and I calculated all that had been lost since that houseware had been set into my hands by my eldest sibling, the current moment not excluded – the current moment the culmination of a desert's sand through my young fingers.

Much, maybe most, of this was my fault – my failure at loving Clare the way I meant to, the way she needed me to, my failure at protecting the things that truly matter, regardless of the force of wind against them.

But even so. At what point do the collective and unintended failings of relationship validate an all-access pass to third parties? When does the sacred bond of intimacy become a line blurred enough for others to cross?

If Keith wasn't guilty of taking full advantage of a wounded relationship, he at least knowingly leaned into its disarray far enough to obscure the view of the two people still attempting to sort through it.

And even if love isn't always fairly won or justly lost; even if fairness is just another fragile accord between us and our own gods – fluid virtues vaulted across our own private skies of stars, the more heart-breaking realization – the one nearly impossible for me to face – was the realization Clare's actions, her decisions, also drove a wedge against reconciliation, also played a part.

I stared at Ben's pot, and its curry mud bath, and realized no matter the direction of any of the damage standing before or behind us, something sacred had been compromised, tarnished – if not by Clare's active choice, in absentia, at least, of her choosing. And that realization brought me pause and made me wonder how my own feelings toward her might shift, might change in response. It was the very last thing I wanted to explore, but there it was – staring back at me, cold.

I took four steps back and leaned against the door frame. The wind puckered my shirt. Clare broke our silence by asking me what the matter was with my leg. She eyed the weight I shifted to my good ankle.

"Twisted it," I answered.

"Again?" she asked.

"Seems my fate."

"When?" she asked.

"Moments ago."

"Here?"

Her momentary concern for me felt rewarding. But I was aware the fortune was fleeting, in this case.

"I fell out of a tree."

"A tree?"

"Your neighbor's tree. That big maple."

"Oh, good lord," sighed Keith. His eyes aimed skyward.

"Hey, Wolfgang," I said. "You think this is easy, you have no idea."

"You climbed their tree?" Clare asked.

"If either of you thinks this is easy..." I said.

Clare placed an open palm across her hip, and her eyes met Keith's, their shared expression illustrative of two people who wished the scene they stood in the middle of would magically evaporate into thin air.

"You scaled that tree to spy on me, and then you fell," Clare said.

"At this very point," I said, "what difference could the sequence of anything possibly matter?"

My ankle throbbed. I imagined it the shape of a small bag of onions, but didn't want to check. Instead, I took a moment to calculate how many one-legged hops it would take to make my way back across the kitchen floor to land a forearm across Keith's mugging face. His former desire to flee the scene was obviously now competing with his renewed thirst to witness the expanding girth of hole into which I could dig myself in front of Clare. If he had a utility shovel with him, he would have speed pitched it to me.

"Look," I finally said, and glanced at Clare before directing my words to Keith. "I'm probably the last person in the world to give advice right now. Or make demands. But I don't know you, and you sure as hell don't know me – anything about me. You may think you do, but you don't."

Keith's expression remained unchanged, impassive.

"And the same is true about me and Clare," I said. "Our relationship. Our failures. Our anything. You want to be her friend, then be her friend. But be careful about putting your hands on things that aren't yours. At least not yet. Or assessing the damage from storms you didn't and don't stand in the middle of."

I paused to allow those words resonance.

"Watch your overreach," I said.

Mind your own fucking talons, I wanted to add but didn't.

And then Clare did something I hadn't expected – she agreed with me.

"This *isn't* about Keith," she said. "This whole mess – it's about you and me."

Despite her qualification of our relationship as a whole mess, her validation of my sentiment threw me. I really hadn't expected anyone to agree with anything I had to say in that moment. And the qualified validation from her gave my heart, finally, the safety net it needed to breathe.

I paused. We all did. I let the enormity of the moment sink in, and then said: "Then maybe you and I should talk, Clare. About us. About the whole mess that isn't about Keith."

Clare nodded, looked straight ahead. And when nothing more was said, Keith finally volunteered to remove himself. "Just let me get my coat," he said.

He grabbed his wool coat from the chair, tucked it under his arm, and angled to the door. He crossed inches from my chest, avoided eye contact, and disappeared. Given everything that came before, it was an unremarkable exit.

After he departed, Clare fell silent. Her head was bowed. She looked close to tears. My heart drummed.

"I mean," she finally said, "that was charming."

"I'm sorry," I said. "But what did you expect?"

"Not this!" she said. "Not, in the least, this. And for the record, Keith and I are just friends."

"People who are just friends don't hold each other the way you two were," I said. "For the record."

"That was a hug," she said. "I don't know what it looked like from the view of the Bosner's backyard maple, but in this kitchen – all that was, was a hug."

I leaned against the wall, felt a wave of wonder, like the orbital path of water molecules birthing and rotating beneath a rampant tide streaming past my two feet.

"Christ, Clare," I said. "I mean, how did we even get here? What are we doing?"

There comes a point when you become stymied by the confluence of events that have pushed your life and body to a precipice or escarpment where you no longer recognize the person you love, much less your own self or any of the options standing before you. And you wonder how you let that happen – how either of you let it happen, the wayward navigation so far afield from where the two of you began. In the wan light of that moment, I barely recognized the both of us.

I listed against the door frame and wondered how long it would take before any of it could be pieced back together.

"We're separated right now, Jack. You and me. We're not together."

"Is that becoming permanent?" I asked.

"It makes no difference what it's becoming. What matters is right now. And right now, you and I are apart. As in, not together. You can't scale trees in my neighbor's backyard and pummel your way through my doorway to change that. It's only ever going to ensure the opposite response."

"Are you in love with this guy?" I asked. My voice caught awkwardly at the tail end of the question.

"In love with him?! With Keith?" she said, and turned toward me, her brow knitted.

"Makes a mean curry – "

"No, I'm not in love with him."

"Because I'm pretty sure he might be with you."

I slid down the jamb and rested on the floor in the open doorway. The breeze felt good against my face; it was the sole thing.

"Jack," she said. "Our lives, regardless of whatever upheaval they're in – they need to be apart from one another, you know?"

"Separate upheavals?" I asked.

I wondered what Clare meant by our lives supposing to be apart from one another. I wondered how similar or different it meant in comparison to being broken up. I wondered about the permanence of either or both.

"We haven't even spoken in weeks," she said.

"Isn't that enough?" I asked.

"No," she said softly, sounding sad. "It isn't enough for me. I'm still trying to figure out my way in all of this."

"In all of what, though?"

"In my own footing forward."

I watched her, silent, unsure of what to say or ask.

"Footing," she added, "that has nothing to do with you."

At that, it was impossible not to feel even more alone, and more aware of the error in judgment I had made initiating my Navy Seal masquerade to her doorstep.

Clare had always been so patient with me, with us. It may have been the one area where she gave too much. She demonstrated seemingly endless reassurance, allowance. All through our relationship, she continually reminded us both of the tensile strength of our connection, her capacity for forgiveness. I don't think I considered, nearly enough, the limitations of that offering. She gave me so little reason to assume, after whatever smoke cleared, she wouldn't be standing there. Beside me.

"I'm not in love with Keith Hollbeck," she said, her eyes locked into mine. "This isn't about that. It's about – finding my own footing.

Forward."

"Forward into what?"

"I don't know yet," she said. "I wish I did."

More than anything else in the world, I found myself longing for honesty, for truth. Even if it hurt. Love first, but truth a close second. The absence of those two bound elements, I realized, would easily be our undoing – anyone's undoing.

"Just tell what's in your heart, then," I said. "What matters most."

Clare nodded.

"And then we'll figure out what to do," I said. "From there."

Clare's eyes welled. She took a moment, and then said, "It's not that easy."

I nodded, and Clare took a deep breath. She stared at the blued concrete and trees outside her window. For a long while, she remained silent, seemingly lost in thought, and her expression slowly shifted, from anger and guardedness into genuine sadness.

"I met you when I was seventeen years old," she said. "And from the moment you walked down those stairs to ask me out, I pictured my whole life alongside yours."

I thought of Clare's face that same night, her red cheeks and wet eyes on the other side of the doorway glass after I descended the stairway, her small, gloved hand spread across the pane, both of us strangers to each other, each lost in wonder of the world that hovered on the other side.

"If you added the time it took me to know," she said. "It would clock in under a minute. That's how long it took. For my heart to open. To you. To us."

I smiled, nodded.

"I'm not even sure your feet landed yet on the last few steps – I knew before you got there."

"Me too," I said

"How did that happen?" she asked. "And why doesn't it happen for anything else? For any other single thing?"

Clare smiled. Separate tears rolled down her face, and she wiped them away in advance of a soft burst of a laugh, acknowledgment of the emotion she had stored away, its honest reveal.

"You probably think I don't even think about all that anymore," she said. "But I do. I know how lucky we were. To have found each other. I know how rare this is."

Clare paused.

"No matter how deep I push it beneath the surface," she said, "it's the one thing that bobs back up."

"Like a seal," I said, and Clare smiled.

"But that's sort of the problem, too," she said. "The ocean of us, the largeness of it."

I waited for her to gather her thoughts. She took her time, and in the waiting my chest, my lungs felt as though they were filling with saline. I wanted to reach for her hand and hold it, tell her how impossible the world was without her in it.

Clare took a breath, exhaled it slowly, and bowed her head a moment and wiped her tears.

"What scares me, Jack," she finally said, "isn't whether or not you and I have a love that's strong enough. What scares me is how ours might be a love I can't be strong enough in."

I nodded, wondered, wished I knew what to ask and how to ask it.

"At least," she said. "I can't be strong enough in it right now."

"Okay," I said. "It's okay, Clare. Just – I don't know where you want me to be. In this, or outside of this. Where do you need me to be?"

"All of us get to a place in our lives where we need to stand on our own two feet," she said. "Where we need to leave home."

"Leave home?"

"Yes," she said. "Home."

That's when I noticed Clare's posture, as though she was summoning courage to open an unfamiliar door. It was the first time I reflected on the duration of transition to which our love, our meeting one another was tethered — the young woman she was when we met, anxious to experience the depths of love, shaken by its challenges, disappointments, her own tentative steps in the face of them, the woman she was moving forward to meet on the other side. She was finding a way to leave home. All these miles away, all these years together, I became the emblem of that home.

I felt at once moved to get out of her way and devastated in knowing I had to.

Clare pulled the long strands of hair from her forehead and tucked them behind her ear.

"Live your life, Jack," she said. "We both simply need to live our lives again. Separate from each other's. Maybe sometime after doing that, we'll both find we can live one together again. But right now, I can't do it. And I can't have you dropping out of neighbor's trees while I'm living mine. So please, if out of nothing more than appreciation of the love we have shared, please respect the place I'm in, and live your life."

She said it as though it was the easiest thing in the world. She said it as though it was even possible.

I took up Clare's suggestion to simply live my life by sleeping three days straight. Or nearly. There were waking moments, but few that involved movement.

I was reasonably certain my current physical condition mirrored a convalescent soldier fetched from shrapnel singed trenches. Minus the flesh wounds and missing body parts. Minus the inability to pee standing up. But in all other realms, I doubted the difference.

I stared at the crawl of the sunlight across the ceiling, the flicker of light and shadow when birds flew past my windows. I listened to the boom of the expanded heating ducts when the furnace kicked on, the whisper of warm air through the vents. And then to the silence that followed.

I touched my fingertips to my eyelids, and moved them lightly across my lips, as if to remember who I was, as to remind myself of my own impossible existence.

There were minutes, hours and days at a time I wished for the fortune of failed breath. Or memory.

Breaking four whole days of silence, the phone rang. Hoping it was Clare, I bounded across the room and hurdled monkey candles and stacked relationship self-help books to answer it. It was Krystoff's voice that came through the ear piece. He asked me to join him in the Scapegoat to set up grizzly hair snag stations.

"Is it time already?" I asked. I knew immediately I was not ready.

"April, son. It's time."

There is no way in hell, I thought. *I'm in absolutely no shape to participate – in anything.*

I verbally stumbled through a series of conjured excuses, none of which found their way to standing firmly on two feet.

"It's the timing," I told Krystoff. "It's not ideal."

"Really?" he said. "Your dance card is filled? With what?"

Krystoff paused, listened with me to the silence.

"That's what I thought," he said. "Look – the biota awaits, dude. Your clumsy footprints across its muddy back."

"How about…would it be possible if I joined a few weeks in?"

"We're heading out day after tomorrow," answered Krystoff without pause. "Jesse and Theresa and I. We need a fourth, so if you're not in the Citgo lot by 5 a.m. Saturday morning, we'll drag your skinny ass through your bedroom window."

Silence.

"Your ass. Your choice."

At this, I smiled. And I imagined the journey to the Scapegoat, envisioned the painful shift into socialization and also, too, the smell of the damp earth thawing. I wondered if I would be ready, wondered if, when I got there, I'd be able to thwart the stronger desire to stray from Krystoff and the others to the sheer outcrops of the higher elevations. I fantasized taking nothing with me but a wood cross and industrial-sized box of ten penny nails. Bereft of all other faculties or resources, I would, at least, possess the cross. And the nails.

Back in the Scapegoat, it took less than five days for the four of us to put each griz hair snag station back in place, the exact same locations of the previous summer.

Those few mornings, we sipped smoky coffee in the wan light, and bitched about new muscle aches and bruises. Dictated by compass and geo maps, we verified coordinates, hiked solo to the station locations, and then wandered back to camp where we drank in cool evenings in repair, our blistered feet near the fire, our mugs topped with wine or tea, our stomachs filled with re-hydrated stews and elbow macaroni. Our bowls steamed past our faces into the boughs of Douglas fir.

Though I spent those nights and my silent hikes through wood mostly contemplating my separation from Clare and what, if any of it, could be put back together again, it felt good being in the open world again, working up a sweat. I watched leopard frogs emerge from the bog-surrounding sedges, garter snakes slip across sun-spliced meadows. The earth surrounding me, in contrast to the immediate mess of my life, continued its hopeful movement toward thaw. And that, at least, provided inspiration.

We spent the last week of April training the new team of study volunteers: Jesse, Theresa and I designated as team leaders. Early May, songbirds returned; yellow warblers, tanagers and bluebirds flitted through branches. The earth smelled new and mossy. Thin clouds of mayflies hovered over the river.

We fanned from our campsite into the cool woods toward taut lines of newly stretched barbed wire. Often, I stepped alone into the colder shadows of trees, closed my eyes and listened for the sound of newly woken bears treading through the mud.

More than ever before, my heart pounded in hope. In need. In everything.

I invited Sumi to a gathering at Krystoff's house, a small cottage on a treed lot split by Rattlesnake Creek. It was a beautiful place, only five miles from the city, but neatly tucked into the woods and silence.

I wondered whether mixing Sumi with the bear study volunteers was a good idea, but Sumi seemed to think it would be fine and welcomed the diversion. She showed up at my doorstep in a white tank top T-shirt beneath a flower-patterned blouse, purple barrettes in her hair, her lips painted red. It was good to see her.

"I'm excited to meet real-life bear trackers," she said on our drive to Krystoff's house.

"Don't I qualify?" I asked.

"You more than qualify," she answered. "But more figurative than literal."

"What does that mean?" I asked.

Krystoff met us at the door. He clutched his perennial quart of chocolate milk in one hand and walking staff in the other. He smiled broadly at Sumi. "New volunteer?" he asked.

"My own personal one. This is my friend, Sumi."

We walked into Krystoff's small cottage, a split log walled living room with a hanging brass light fixture, one wall covered in a series of black and white photos of bears, mostly griz. In the kitchen, a handful of volunteers stood around the open bottles of wine. They discussed Chico Hot Springs and the local Pioneer league baseball team, the Missoula Osprey.

Sumi and I assumed a place on the periphery. We sipped spiked cider and nibbled from paper plates the stuffed chipotle peppers Krystoff had prepared, smoky, cheesy half-moons drenched in peppery gravy.

We took turns joining in the conversation and breaking to wander across the dark lawn to stare at the creek and the night sky that winnowed across its back.

The party soon stretched from the kitchen into the living room. Krystoff's cats snaked through our legs and bounded across the backs of chairs and the sofa. Candlelight swam holes through the fog of smoke.

Sumi continually filled her glass. She alternated between hard cider and white wine, and became more comfortable with her newly introduced social circle. I watched her meander between the others. She slapped her hand against her knee or on the floor in laughter. Soon she listed, and then leaned against the wall. A crooked smile weighed her mouth, her eyes cast downward. She nodded her head at the conversation near her.

"Are you okay?" I asked.

"I'm beautiful."

I was mid-conversation with Jesse about the early summer progression of our research, when I spotted Sumi struggle around a corner and lose her balance. Her wine glass spiraled toward the floor, broke at impact into a dance of clear shards. The gathering hushed a moment and turned toward her. A couple of people applauded.

Sumi held herself up, one hand splayed neatly against the facing wall, her elbow locked. She attempted a smile.

I excused myself from Jesse and grabbed a dustpan from Krystoff's kitchen and swept the glass shards into a nest.

"You're so good," Sumi said. "Maybe I've tarnished your reputation here."

"It's only glass," I answered. "There are worse things to break."

After I emptied the glass fragments into the garbage and returned, Sumi's face had lost color.

"Pointing me toward the bathroom would be good," she said. When I reached for the handle and found it locked, Sumi sighed and then turned on the balls of her feet and rushed out the front screen door and across the porch. I followed her out into the lawn.

From the cottage, I watched Sumi's moon-illuminated tank top weave between the shadowed trees. I saw her silhouette bend toward the earth. I had a feeling she was throwing up.

I gave her some time and then walked toward her. She was back on her feet. She wove toward me. Her small hands wiped away tears.

"Oh, that's impressive," she said.

I smiled. "No one noticed," I said.

Sumi slung her arm around a white pine for balance. She took a few breaths and then lowered herself to the sod. She rested her head on the top of her peaked knees. I took off my sweatshirt and draped it over her shoulders.

"Aw," she said. "That's nice. Chivalry lives!"

"Are you okay?"

"I'll be okay," she answered. "I'm continually finding alternative versions of okay, and this is just another one of them hobbling down the gangplank."

I sat next to her, and she leaned her head against my shoulder. I sensed the rise and fall of her breathing. I kissed the warm top of Sumi's head. Her hair smelled like summer. We listened to the creek, the wind through trees, and the soft murmur of the party laughter and conversations behind us.

Sumi pointed her nose toward the stars.

"I love this sky when it's this color," she said. "Exactly this color."

I followed her gaze, up through the trees. A half dozen swallows swooped over the creek, and then back up against the amber horizon. It was the first I realized we had consumed nearly a full evening and were already flirting with morning.

"It only lasts a short while," she said. "And then disappears."

"We should get you home," I said.

I patted her knee and stood. Sumi remained by the tree, seated.

"You're over this, already?" she asked.

"Over it?"

"Because I'm not over anything," she said. "My new theory is overs don't exist."

"Overs? Sumi, it's like five in the morning…"

"Everybody wants to get over *some*thing," she said. "Some broken heart or horribly cruddy thing. Slings and arrows – our own Shake-spearean shit storm. But what if there isn't a getting over? Of the big things – the heart split across the center things? What if there's only forgetting or remembering? Those are your two options."

"Forgetting or remembering."

"Two flavors only – take your pick. Remembering – that one hurts like hell and gets you where, I don't know. And forgetting, well, that's a whole different soup. It means discarding the people and things that made you, shedding chunks of who you are. Your life experience in a series of boxes on the shelf."

"Isn't there also…healing?" I asked. "As an option?"

"Journeyman's jargon for amnesia," she said.

"Are you always this verbose when you're drunk?" I asked. "Philosophical?"

"If you only knew the bowl of fish swimming my thoughts twenty-three hours a day," she said. "Alcohol just spills them over the rim."

I filled my lungs and breathed out with pursed lips, inflated cheeks. And then I knelt beside her, sat and stared at the handful of stars barely visible.

"I have no fucking idea what any of the answers are," I said. "I'm just trying to keep from falling into about a million pieces. At any given time."

Sumi placed her hand in mine. "Forget about that," she said. "The rambling, incoherent sermon of mine back there. Just me reminding myself some things aren't answerable. Some conflicts don't have tidy little conclusions rattling around at the bottom of their boxes. Meantime, there's a whole world surrounding us. One that doesn't exactly jog in place while we spin our wheels wondering about everything else."

"At least your wheels are spinning," I said. "Mine are just careening down the passing lane toward the median."

Sumi smiled. She stifled a laugh.

She was right, of course – about that world surrounding us. Conversation like ours reminded me the lost place I remained, and how long I'd been swimming in my own private Black Sea, no longer eying the shore, no longer even believing one existed. No matter where I went or what I did, I failed to stem the constant memory of Ben and Clare, the alluvial river through my veins – Clare's soft kisses and Ben's firm hands on my shoulder, their missed smiles and laughter. I think I found my way into believing they would always be there, consuming me, never letting me go. I somehow believed it had become my job to swim beside them, their memory, their ghosts, because that exercise beat the alternative – swimming forever without them.

"Between your two options," I said, "it turns out remembering is the only one I'm good at."

"Even when it comes to the people who walked away from you on their own two feet?"

"Even when," I said.

"You can't stop your head and heart from going where they go," said Sumi. "But you can give yourself a break from it. Once in a while. A day. Two. An hour. It's okay to take a holiday from thinking everything to death – from remembering. Especially from the people working so hard at forgetting you."

Sumi's face basked in the morning's first trace of sunlight.

She held my hand all the way back to my truck, and then during our drive back to my apartment. She leaned against me when I unlocked the door, my sweatshirt still draped over her shoulders. She walked through the living room into the bedroom. When I returned from the kitchen with a large glass of water and a handful of aspirin that I would force her to swallow, she had stripped to her underwear.

She gulped the aspirin and water, and we folded ourselves beneath the covers; Sumi tucked her knees into her chest. She faced me, her hair splayed across her face.

"How do you feel?"

"Better," she said. She placed her hand on my shoulder. "I feel good here."

I turned off the bedside light. Morning sunlight lit the window frame and stretched across the ceiling.

When she moved closer, I felt her warmth along my body, her breath against my neck. For the longest while, I simply held her. When she pressed her mouth against mine, I felt myself leaning into the newness of it, the texture of her lips, the taste of her mouth, the warmth and wetness familiar and foreign at once, the distinct sensation of otherness. In the oddest way, I felt myself falling against Sumi's kiss, my whole body trembling and warmed, as if to realize the impression, the difference, as if to remember Clare's by the contrast, the separate impressions of comfort and heartbreak wreathed in an increasingly fragile, impossible, marriage.

part four

Holding a piglet is like holding a bear cub. You scratch their tummies and they calm down and look at you as if you might somehow belong together.

Jim Harrison, Returning to Earth

KRYSTOFF DIDN'T OFFICIALLY GRANT ME permission to remain at the Carmichael Cabin all summer. It started gradually. I packed an extra layer of clothing. Then another. I stored extra packets of soup mix, boxes of saltines, jars of peanut butter. I made excuses to stay on past the tracking weekend: trail repair, hair snag station maintenance. The extra days stretched to the following weekend. Then the next. Somewhere along the way, Krystoff accepted I had no plans to return to Missoula until the study concluded. Eventually he took advantage of it and asked me to record field notes in the days between hair sample collections.

I kept a notebook, small enough to stash in my pocket, and scribbled or sketched every plant I came across I was reasonably sure held a place on the grizzly bear's menu – dandelions, shooting stars, the whole smörgåsbord of wild berries – soap, huckle, straw, salmon, mountain ash, rasp – and the white-bark pine nuts, army cutworm moths, dogtooth violets, cow parsnip, horsetails, pea vine, clover and mountain sorrel.

I had a split purpose – provide Krystoff with enough data he continued to look the other way when the others returned to Missoula while I remained behind – that was my cover. But my primary goal, the one hidden from everyone else, was my desire to fully and finally prove the possibility of human hibernation. It was the single hope I clung to. If I could avoid consciousness but keep the muscle in my chest beating over a sustained duration, maybe then I could survive the time it took Clare to decide whatever it was she was deciding. And if her eventual conclusion was the one I feared above and beyond my own death, maybe I could keep just this one escape hatch forever at arm's length away, should I need to dive through its opening.

Human hibernation was my out. Beneath the subnivian zone and the cold blanket of debris, under the layer of elk bones and antlers and leaf mold, deep enough into the earth even Ben and Clare's memories would strain to find me, maybe there I could give my lopsided heart temporary, if not permanent, rest. If I could understand how bears fed themselves, how their diet and behavior patterns shifted across seasons, maybe I could find the same path as theirs beneath the winter stars.

The study was one thing – the fragment-by-fragment formation of bear densities, survival rates, territory shift. But the possibility of my own aortal rest, uninterrupted sleep – that was the end game that captured the whole of my imagination.

As the summer chewed on, I tracked the pulse of my resting heart rate. And nearly every night, the time between heartbeats stretched farther and farther apart, like boats loosened from their moorings, drifting out to sea.

I had my mouth filled with oatmeal, early morning, and Krystoff bounded through the cabin door as he often did mid-week, short on breath.

"How we doing?" he asked.

I poured us both mugs of black coffee, and we sipped them outside the cabin. We held the tin mugs at chest level in between sips. The steam drifted up into our faces.

"Weather looks like we're in for rain," he said. "Could be a stretch of it."

I had noticed a fall in the air pressure, but I didn't yet trust my awareness of such things.

"We should probably take a long hike to check on things," he continued. "Might be the last chance for a while."

Krystoff and I hiked the path of hair snag stations. Along the way, we took breaks and watched antic shoals of cutthroat trout responding to the mid-day hatches while beefy salmon flies bounced against our foreheads and chests. We spotted dusky brown ptarmigan fanned from field bushes, and listened to the piercing whistle of hoary marmots, their snouts twitching in the cover of rocks.

It was a beautiful late July day, clear skies and slight breeze. The sun felt good when we hiked the open stretches along the river.

"This girl came to see me at my office," said Krystoff. He re-tied his bootlaces and rested against a boulder.

I turned toward him.

"Sumi, I think her name was?"

"Oh?"

"Wasn't she the young woman you brought to the party at my place?" he asked. "Last spring?"

"The same one."

"She was asking about you. Wondering how you were."

"Did you tell her?"

"I told her you were in the Scapegoat, compiling research."

"That seem to satisfy her?"

"Could be," said Krystoff.

We resumed our walk. I could hear the cascading water of the North Fork Falls.

"It's none of my business," Krystoff said. He lifted his eyebrows. "But this girl asking about you was wearing a wedding ring."

"We're friends," I said. "Don't let your imagination run any further than that."

"Sounds like some fodder for the campfire," he said.

We walked on, passed Sarbo Creek Canyon, and took note of the condition of the hair snag stations along the flood plain. We hiked to

Dobrota Creek and then turned back, the sun high above our shoulders. By the time we made it back to the cabin, a hued roil of clouds blotted the horizon.

Krystoff's prediction was accurate; it rained, off and on, mostly on, for the next six days. Some rains fell hard – sweeping, driving rains that transformed the terrain, swelled rivers, washed trails into muddy soup and filled bogs to capacity. Mostly, I holed up in the cabin. I kept a low-grade fire going in the wood stove, lined up cook pans and cups under the various leaks in the ceiling; they collected rainwater that seeped through the shingles and rafters.

Even though I was captive, for the first time all summer, I failed to feel restless. I felt calm. I watched the rainy world through the open doorway, the continual fall of precipitation through the trees, the sweep of winds that sometimes tousled and bowed evergreen. I was content to watch and wait. I boiled water and drank tea. I wrote letters to Clare that I carefully set in the fire at night, page upon page. I waited things out.

Nestled in the cupboard of the Carmichael Cabin, stashed behind an empty biscuit tin, I pulled free a foot tall pine cask of a mysterious source of potential libation. The words *Chartreuse V.E.P. vieillissement exceptionnellement prolongé* along with a star-emblazoned cross were burned into the panel that lifted to reveal a liter-sized amber glass bottle with a wax-bathed cork. The bottle had been opened, but remained nearly full. I pulled the cork and smelled what I imagined a conifer tree basted in kerosene would offer.

Whatever vieillissement exceptionnellement prolongé meant, I decided I could use some.

I poured myself a thimble sized glass and held it to the light. A neon green hued liquid with dark herb flecks swam in the incandescence. I closed my eyes and tipped the glass to my lips, waited a second, and then gulped it into my stomach. A warm ember spread immediately across my chest.

Whoever these Frenchmen were who created this pine cone elixir, I was eternally grateful for their fortitude and ingenuity. Sometimes you find yourself alone in the wilderness and tangentially bonded with people with whom you hold no singular possibility of contact. This was that.

I downed two more swallows and vowed to nurse what remained over time.

When the shift of rain finally ended, it revealed crisp blue skies and unwavering sun. I had to wait two days for the trails to dry out; they had turned, mostly, to mud. I scavenged storm-downed wood and set the limbs in the sun to dry. The earth smelled of moss and cedar. I washed my clothes in the creek and hung them on the line. In the sunlight, I watched steam lift from the roof shingles and from the reeds and sedges along the river, liberated moisture that merged into sky.

I pulled my pick-up truck alongside a pay phone in Lincoln, a block from the market. When first answering, my brother Alex's voice always sounded as though he had swallowed a fish tank of gravel.

"Did I wake you?" I asked.

"It's like ten o'clock."

"I know. Just asking."

"Where are you?"

"Montana. Still Montana. At a pay phone."

"Everything okay?"

"More or less. Mostly less…but, you know…everything is a work in progress."

"Sometimes the wheels fall off, though," my brother said. "And then it becomes a tough call what's progress and what's disaster."

"Do you think about him, a lot?" I asked, more abruptly than I thought I would.

"Ben?"

"Yes. Ben."

"With Ben, I mean, there's no way you couldn't."

"I don't know how…I don't always know how we're supposed to think about him. How we're supposed to miss him."

"There aren't any supposed to's."

"Not that – how to let go of him. I don't know how to let go of him."

"Who said we had to?"

"Because I don't know how else to see him again. How are we supposed to see him again? Just the him he was – the unique person he was, without the loss of him, the sadness of missing him, getting in the way? I don't want that to forever remain larger than who he was."

"Yeah, that," answered Alex. "I don't know."

We both paused, breathed.

"What's going on out there, anyway?" Alex asked. "Are you staying permanently or something?"

"Not permanently. I'm sure not that. I have no idea how long, though."

"What's going on with Clare?"

"I don't know…That – I *really* don't know."

Alex was silent. I pictured his facial expression as he attempted to form his follow-up question. For Alex, putting together the follow-up question took the concentration of an origami master, a simple inquiry suddenly seeming as intricate as folded swan. The question was there. You had to wait for him to fold all the corners in first.

"I miss them both – Ben and Clare," I said. "And it keeps getting harder than the other way around."

"Yeah," said Alex. "Well…"

"I should go, Alex. Sorry for this. Just – I wanted to, you know, hear your voice and… I wish to hell we were in the same room and could, I don't know, open a bottle of something, like Ben would."

"Me too," he answered. "Hey, Jack…this isn't, you know, none of this is easy. Knowing how to… move past it, how to remember without missing, or whatever."

"I know."

"And it's easier to keep it to yourself because you feel like nobody gets it."

"I know. I know."

"But I do get it. I get it, too."

"Thanks, Alex."

"You know the image I keep thinking of, as a way to explain it? Remember Wally Coyote?"

"Wile E. Coyote?"

"That cartoon coyote that was always trying to murder The Road Runner."

"Wile E. E was just his middle initial."

"His first name was Wile?"

"Yes."

"I mean who would name…whatever that coyote's name was – he'd hide a cannon pointed toward The Road Runner's jogging trail or something and, when The Road Runner didn't show up, he'd wander toward the bluff looking for him and accidentally trip the cannon, and the cannon ball would missile through his own torso right before The Road Runner sped around the corner beeping him out of the way."

"Something like that."

"He tottered through the cloud of The Road Runner's dust with this perfectly round hole torn through him. And with this seasick expression. You could see the sky through the hole."

My brother was eternally open-minded when it came to source material to illustrate life philosophy, Chuck Jones animation not excluded.

"That's how it feels," he said. "You can function – your feet and hands work. The world is the same. There's virtually nothing changed. But you have a cannon ball hole ripped through the middle of who you were."

I pictured myself walking the world with a foot-wide hole through my torso, my rib cage fissured from the raised letters of ACME.

"Except for that," I said. "A cannon ball through our torsos, I guess we'll be okay."

"Half the time," said Alex. "I'm convinced we're nothing more than mother-fucking cartoon characters."

When I hung up the phone and listened to my quarter fall into the pay phone clutch, I tried to imagine how Alex envisioned the merging of our cartoon character lives with the real ones. If half our lives were cartoons, what were they in the other half?

As summer progressed, warm days and light breezes, soft clouds of mayflies and caddis, I became more and more at home with the wilderness surrounding me. I felt myself merging with the sub-Alpine fir, the boulder-strewn meadows, the cluttered stands of white bark pine, the springs and seeps overgrown with Alpine willow.

Some trails I knew by heart and could walk in my sleep, the ravines and charred treed openings beneath the Flint Mountain Palisades, the warm, open meadows, the canyon switchbacks, flanked by red shale, the swaying grass valleys, spruce bottomland forests, vest-pocket meadows, the silted bogs, and feeder streams – it got to the point I could navigate them in the dark.

I continued to piece together the patterns of the grizzly, their movement revealed through paw prints, overturned boulders, and claw marks wrapped around tree trunks. Each new shred of evidence helped me piece together their patterns – activity that spiked when the humidity swelled and during the first week of a new moon and then all but disappeared when strong winds filled the mountain pass or when the moon's girth swelled.

With every puzzle piece locked into place, I felt an ever emerging calm. In contrast to the first days of early summer when I arrived and spent my days hiking in as many directions as I could, wanting to see all that surrounded me, anxious to consume every ounce of it, I now took my time exploring a more immediate perimeter. I learned the plant life, the shale and the rock, the fall of sunlight through the trees, one section of trail at a time. More than anything, the calm I experienced, its sanctuary, stemmed from immersing myself in the rhythm of the world surrounding me.

Finding rhythm. That's how I started to see my time in the woods. It's the one thing that staved off the hurt of Clare's abandonment. When I relaxed enough to remain still. When I stopped wanting more than the sun above me, the wind through trees.

The absence of Ben and Clare, my missing them, still pressed against my skin, still hurt. But I felt less urgency to restrain the emotion of loss. It became a sensation I learned to let walk alongside me, along the riverbank, through the copse of trees, simply another layer of my meandering being.

There were two moons in August. Between them, the sky held long stretches of clouds, clouds whose undersides were saturated, nearly matching the hue of the scorched earth beneath them. I swam beneath the month's second waxing moon and heard a thrashing through the woods above the riverbank – scratching and clawing loud enough you could hear it over the river's current.

I climbed the shoreline. My chest heaved when I stood.

The thrashing continued, the sound of branches being torn from trees, determined peals of wood and splintered bark. When these sounds ceased, I heard footsteps against the earth.

I hiked up the bank. I ran my hands over rock, hoisted my body and placed my bare feet over the ones with sturdy enough landing, and was careful not to loosen anything on my climb that would give away my presence.

I stood motionless on the upper bank. The river swirled and gulped beneath me. The trees were black.

The mystery animal stopped its foraging. For a while there was only silence, just my heart pumping against the muscles of my chest.

I heard a guttural snort and looked for breath climbing into sky.

Nearly every night, I swam the river. And when I did, I believed bears watched me from above. In my imagination, they collected along the bank and stared as my body pulled against the river's current. With my skin bronzed from summer sun, my form blurred by the water, maybe they'd mistake me for one of their own.

Each time I swam to the bank to rest, my body wet, gulping breath, I'd sit on the rocks and wonder when they'd come, what was taking them so long. I imagined the fraternity and warmth I'd feel as I set my chin, my lips, into the curve of their muzzled necks.

By summer's end, we had collected enough griz hair samples, we could, as Jesse stated, fully reconstruct one whole bear. Our paper envelopes contained a myriad of gold and silver and brown strands and were neatly filed into boxes, snag station numbers and dates marked across each one: the story of spring and summer bear migration through the Scapegoat Wilderness awaiting reassembly, sample by sample, a steamer trunk of bear hair follicles, six times as many as the summer before.

The last weekend of September, a cool front descended the Scapegoat, purple scudded clouds, frost-kissed leaves and blades of grass. We made our final sample collection trek, held our last communal bonfire at Carmichael Cabin. The spiral of smoke and flame reached through branches.

The other volunteers recalled stories of their summer experience, bear sightings, wasp stings and a few close calls with navigation, and I sat on a boulder near the trees, apart from the others, my knees tucked into my chest. I felt the fire's distant warmth against my skin, and I stared at the stars.

Krystoff had asked me to stay on an additional week to help deconstruct the snag stations and pack out, but I had already solidified my plan to remain in the Scapegoat well beyond that. Even with the turning weather, the last place I was ready to return to was Missoula.

After the volunteers packed up and hiked out the next day, the coals of the fire bed sifted smoke, and I placed birch bark and dried branches across it, kindled a fresh fire and waited for night.

I hiked off through McDonnell Meadow, through a cool grove of sub-Alpine fir, the scree slopes above tinted blue in the moon. Stars flecked the surface of a small kettle pond, through copses of aspen, and leaves fluttered in the night wind. I climbed carefully down the slope of rock and spruce that passed the wicker dams of the feeder creeks and fanned into the banks of the Blackfoot.

I swam against the river's current, the moon above me. I imagined I could feel it, the moon, like a cold, open palm across my shoulder blades.

Past the current, past the friction of my body through the water, I could hear their movement through the woods. They moved closer, their long claws against scree and duff, the snap of twigs beneath their steps, the sonorous whisper of their collected breath, above the river, its communal cloud flowering into sky.

The following week-end, Krystoff dumped empty spools across the picnic table, canvas bags and nylon frame packs.

"We'll fan out at Dobrota," he said. "Wind up barbed wire like forked spaghetti. You take the east stations; I'll take the west."

We met back at Carmichael Cabin at dusk, three quarters of the stations now fully removed, all traces packed and loaded into Krystoff's van. We'd get the remaining stations in the morning.

We sat by the fire and sipped tin mugs of steaming chicken and stars soup. I retreated to the cabin and pulled the Chartreuse elixir from the cupboard and poured Krystoff a neat shot and set it on the bench next to him.

"You unearthed the motherfucker!" he said and grabbed the bottle.

"Wait," I said. "This is yours?"

He held the half empty bottle toward the rising moon.

"Not anymore," he said.

"Oops," I said.

"Don't sweat it."

Krystoff handed me the bottle.

"Grain alcohol is as good a stipend as anything else," he said, and explained the green liqueur I had been nursing these past many weeks was the invention of a group of monks huddled in a monastery in the Chartreuse Mountains of Grenoble, France – a carefully guarded recipe nearly four centuries old and counting.

"Four centuries?" I said. "Talk about your vows of silence."

Krystoff gulped the shot, and in the same motion, extended his empty glass toward my hand clutching the bottle. We downed a couple more pours in short order, and I told Krystoff I was planning on staying on past the weekend.

"How long?" he asked. "You've been up here all summer."

"A while," I said. "Not sure."

Krystoff tipped the bottle to his glass one more time and poured it. He held the glass to his lips and paused.

"How long exactly?" he asked. "A week or so?"

"No" I said. "Longer."

He drank the Chartreuse with his eyes closed.

"Sometime you're going to have to tell me the whole story," he said.

"Story?"

"It's about a girl, I imagine."

I paused. "I imagine," I said.

"The one that visited me, asking about you?"

"Not her."

"Right, right," he said. "It's never about the ones asking about us. It's usually about the ones that don't."

We listened to the fire hiss into a wet strip of wood.

"Did I ever tell you about the first time I was charged by a griz?" Krystoff asked.

"Maybe."

"I did the one thing you're not supposed to do. I ran. Up a tree."

"You did?"

"This female griz was sucking huckleberries off of branches, happy as a clam, when I came lumbering through the meadow and startled the Christ out of both of us at once."

"Shit."

"She turns toward me, shifts her weight, moves her lips, opens her jaw. She only hesitates a moment and false charges twice, and then breaks the Christ out on a full out gait."

Krystoff took another swig, this one straight from the bottle, wiped his mouth with the back of his hand and winced.

"I mean, you never saw anything like – here comes Mama Bear, lips purple with huckleberry juice, running at the rookie biologist who is busy shitting the canvas out of his pants. I was maybe twenty years old."

"What did you do?"

"I ran the fuck for this spruce and dry humped the thing all the way up. Only, the spruce I chose was actually between me and the charging bear. So with my nuts in my larynx, and against every instinct left inside me, for a brief moment of my life on earth, I was actually charging toward a charging bear."

"Oh, shit."

Krystoff beamed.

"And the griz didn't shoot up the tree after you?"

"Does my ass look like it's been re-sewed to my spine? The bear veered. Altogether, last minute. Not that I would've blamed her if she had taken the opportunity, instead, to school me on my fucking manners."

"Close call," I said.

We chortled and sighed. We watched the smoke curl up into the trees.

"I'm staying through the fall," I told him. "Maybe longer."

Krystoff looked at me, waited.

"I want to try something," I said, "Something I don't think anyone has done before. At least not here. Not on purpose."

Still silence.

"Science experiment. You'd appreciate that, right?"

"I'm all ears, Jack."

"There's this thing I learned to do. I don't know, some time ago. It has to do with slowing my heart rate. On command."

"Okay…"

"Nearly in half."

"Half?" he said. "You have a stash of cannabis in the cabin here you haven't told me about?"

"You've heard the term suspended animation, right?" I asked, and found it suddenly difficult to thwart an Alex-inspired image of Wile E. Coyote stepping off a cliff, the moment he hovers mid-air.

"Jack," said Krystoff. "Maybe we should, I don't know – whistle up the dogs, clean out the rest of the stations tomorrow and get our sorry asses back to 'zoula."

"You know about Anna Bågenholm, right?" I asked. "The Norwegian skier? She was submerged in that icy river for more than an hour. Her body temperature was – what, thirty degrees below normal when they pulled her free? Pulled her back into the world unharmed."

"I mean that was – "

"And that little kid in Alberta who wandered out into the freezing night."

"It was actually Saskatchewan," said Krystoff.

"By the time they found her, her heart had stopped beating for nearly two hours."

"Jack," said Krystoff, and then he paused with the bottle toward the fire, its emerald glow washed across his hands. In waiting, I wondered whether I should tell him, also, about the bears I sensed had been watching me from the ridge above the cabin at night, the plumes of their frosted breath. I suddenly wanted to share the entire experience. Every last detail. It pooled rapidly toward the surface.

"I've studied grizzlies thirty-two years straight," he said. He stared up into sky. "Every year, I learn something new. About bears."

"I bet."

"And after all these years," he said, "I've already dispelled nearly every major misconception formerly held in place by the majority of the population. I've watched these animals do amazing things, contemplative or playful acts I don't think most people would even imagine. I've watched them shit, shower and hump. I've seen them mourn, turn tail, and stand their ground. And I can attest, after thirty-two years standing waist deep in the woods and muck alongside them, about ninety-eight percent of all their actions are directly motivated by two things. Just two."

"What two?" I asked.

"Any guesses?"

"Don't tell me sex is one of them," I said. I envisioned Freud in a bear suit.

"Fear and food. In that order."

I looked at him, nodded.

"Fear and food," he repeated. "All but two percent of their daily activity directly related to those two things. Bet you wouldn't have guessed that."

"Food," I answered. "I mean, that's obvious."

Krystoff smiled. "But not fear. Especially not for a mammal formidable enough to be named grizzly."

"I wouldn't have guessed it as the primary motivator," I answered.

"When you stare into that truth deep enough," continued Krystoff, "you start asking yourself whether your own motivations stray far from theirs. What's your food? What's your fear? And how are they changing your movement, shifting your trajectory? Sometimes the things that feed us and the things we fear, they take us way off course."

I smirked, unsure of where Krystoff was going with this.

"You've done a great job of anchoring things up here," he said. "You've added a consistent dimension to the study we wouldn't have had otherwise. I'm appreciative. And it's cool you're immersing yourself in all this goddamned, beautiful wilderness, drinking it in. But don't force your stay in these woods to end in – I don't know what. Folly, for instance."

"Folly?"

"Whatever's going on with you, this girl, or whatever. Be careful about staying here too long, Jack. Be careful about staying for the wrong reasons. Pretty soon, winter is going to fall against this place like a linebacker on top of a ping pong player, and a Montana winter at these altitudes is a whole different shitaree."

Krystoff paused.

"Do you want her to wonder where you had gone and come find you?" he asked. "Is that what this is? Or are you thinking if you lock your body into the snowbank a month solid and turn yourself into a banquet ice sculpture she'll hear about it and miss you? Or if you freeze to death, you'll be lionized or something?"

"Lionized?"

"You know – revered in death?"

"Maybe bearized," I said.

"Because that's, you know, not the optimum relationship outcome: living girl, doornail dead boy. It's fraught with serious limitations."

"Don't oversell it," I said.

"You really can't, and I mean this, can't turn yourself into a fucking bear! Even bears can't do it sometimes, you know? And I don't think you should – I don't know, Walt Disney yourself into an ice cube to find that out. I mean, what in the fuck?"

"Sometimes you need to run toward the charging bear in order to escape him," I said.

"No," answered Krystoff. "Sometimes you need to run up a tree to escape him. The location of the tree, toward or away from the bear, is incidental."

Krystoff packed up, and I pretended to as well. I gathered my things into a duffel bag. But when he readied himself for the hike out, I told him I was going to spend a couple hours fishing the Blackfoot before I followed suit.

"There's a caddis hatch simmering," I said. "I'll see you in Missoula."

I made a furtive hike through the trees, along the Blackfoot, all the way to where South Creek bit into it, some five miles – far enough away, I felt assured Krystoff wouldn't second-guess leaving me and hike back to find me. I passed the pocked mud flats and finger meadows, slopes flanked by sheer rock outcrops and ringing cold feeder streams. I sat on the bank, my fly rod beside me, unassembled. It felt a little strange to realize I was now truly alone.

The study had ended. And Krystoff and I parting on awkward terms, that didn't make it any easier.

I regretted I didn't do a better job explaining my experiment to him. I should have taken the time and care necessary to convince him I was aware there was no way I could replicate the complete winter physiology of bears. Delusion has its limits. I should have made it clear I understood there's no getting around the human hydration factor. Or our own anti- dote to nitrogen build-up – the production of urea that would turn our own bodies into toxic marshes of sludge if we didn't routinely pee it away. There's a long list of metabolic wonders the human body is incapable of – feats a bear accomplishes effortlessly across whole winters of slumber, from sustained bone density and muscle mass to seemingly impossible kidney adaptations. I got that.

Krystoff likely believed I had lost all semblance of sanity.

But, what if part of it *was* possible? Sustained human torpor, if not hibernation? The boot locker of biology texts I horded in the cabin led me to believe hydrogen sulfide could potentially be an untapped resource, the key to the magic kingdom of winter rest. Maybe that one element could help us bridge the difference between surviving nights buried in the soil and morphing into human bomb pops. Hydrogen sulfide was the same chemical mice breathed, bound with oxygen, during their own self-induced torpor. Humans used it, too, as a metabolic stabilizer for our core body temperatures. So, if we are capable of producing it, what if that was the periodic table miracle that preserved the life of the skier submerged in the icy river? The child lost in the snow? What if a gradually reduced heart rate combined with a natural trigger for hydrogen sulfide was the combination necessary to reverse human metabolic quiescence? A night? Two nights? A month?

It would have been helpful to hear from Krystoff if he believed it was at least possible. Not that he would have endorsed my experiment. Just to hear a maybe. Then, at least I'd know there was a chance my skewed plan had promise, the possibility I could reverse my nightly journey of dreaming of bears into the one of bears dreaming.

I was sleeping when the storm clouds knotted across the river. Bursts of lightning illuminated the shadows of trees across the cabin wall and woke me. Their electric crackle was loud enough, I imagined I could smell the lightning's sulfur. Others sounded miles away, like drum beats in the distance. I listened to the rain pelt the roof shingles, the wind bend the trees.

I dreamt myself flowing through the cold, arcing current of the river, the peals of lightning the guttural yowls of bears.

Hours later, I parted the doorway with my knee, and the Scapegoat Massif was white with snow.

Early October, and I was sitting on the cabin porch, sipping vegetable broth, when I spotted her form move through the hemlock. From the rise above the trail, I watched grasshoppers spit through the tall grasses in front of her movement. With a purple backpack over her shoulder and matching shoelaces, I concluded it was Sumi well before she made it to the cabin.

"Holy mother of god!" she said, her voice breathy. "That's a hike. I thought I was lost three or four times. Kept thinking I'd end up at the base of some tree, the Christmas buffet for ferrets."

"What are you doing here?" I asked, astonished to see her.

"No hello first?" she asked. "I've hiked damned near seven miles."

It was the first time I had seen her wearing eyeglasses. They were simple black frames. Her dark hair was pulled back over her ears with purple rubber bands. I moved toward her and noticed the perspiration across her forehead, threads of matted hair against her skin. We hugged. Her small form lifted into the hollow of my chest, warm and soft.

"This is a huge surprise," I said. I handed her a green bandanna from my pocket. She dabbed her forehead and smiled.

"It's been like half a year, now," she said. "I was hoping, A, I'd find you alive and B, that you'd recognize me."

"And C?"

"That you'd be happy to see me if yes to A and B."

"C, then," I said, and wondered how different I must have looked to Sumi all these months later, my hair and beard long and blonded out, my skin bronzed. "How in the hell did you even find me?"

"Had some help with that," she said, and handed me a folded, inked map and directions in a hand I recognized as Krystoff's. "He's hoping you haven't succumbed to teeth of bears," she said. "Or anything else."

"Krystoff," I said. "He thinks I'm veering off the deep end."

"He thinks you're sad, or something. I don't know. But he – he really does hope you're okay."

Sumi dabbed her forehead with the bandanna and handed it back me. "Are you okay?" she asked.

"As okay as ever," I answered.

"Good," she said and nodded. "Good, then."

She sat on the cabin steps, the sun across her shoulders. She set her backpack at her feet and withdrew a carrot cake protein bar from her bag. She peeled the wrapper. "Have one?"

I took it from her hand, and she plunged into her pack for a second one.

After she rested, I gave Sumi a short tour of the wilderness surrounding the cabin, the now slightly withered Dobrota and Eagle Creeks, the view of Crow Peak, the charred spires of trees, the scorched moraine of the Canyon Creek fire. Our boots were black from the sooty soil we tramped across. We counted a half dozen mountain goats dotting the massif, twice as many elk pushing through the headwaters below. The sub-Alpine trail was cool in the shadows and smelled of dewed fern.

"My god," said Sumi. "This place is...wow. One huge wow."

When we returned to the cabin, I revived the fire. Its flames seared the flesh of newly split birch.

"We had this place in the woods where I thought we were happy," I told her.

The moonlight washed our skin blue. Wind whispered through pine.

"Here?" Sumi asked. "Montana?"

"No. Before here," I answered. "It was a small cabin in the woods. A converted storage unit on a Minnesota lake, more a retreat for me than for the two of us, but she joined me out there all the time. The first summer, the leaves were so green through the wide glass doors and through the small round window near the ceiling. The air smelled sweet after it rained. We used to listen to it from bed, never in a hurry to do much more. And Clare was tan from all the summer sun. I mean, we didn't do a whole lot. We'd fall asleep in the breeze of the lake."

"Sounds nice," she said. "Peaceful."

"We decorated the place with a green and blue Mexican blanket we had brought all the way from Taos two summers before. I hung black and white photos I had taken of Clare across the wall." I remembered them as I spoke, Clare posing in the gutted train depot in Minneapolis, her long wool coat, her pretty face through the broken windowpanes.

"But that whole period of time, the retreat by the lake – it wasn't what I thought it was – a time of healing, of taking breaths, of finding our footing. It probably was for me. But it wasn't for her. And I didn't notice."

"It sounds like you were taking time you needed," said Sumi. "A reprieve. And, it's not like any of us map our estrangements out in advance or on purpose. If that's what you're thinking."

"I wasn't mapping *anything* – that's the problem. I wasn't aware of anything beyond my own two feet. And barely them. Least of all, her."

"You forgot her," said Sumi. "You took two or twenty steps away and forgot to weigh her needs with the same grain as your own."

"I did," I said. "At least for a while."

"So does everyone, Jack. It's maybe the one guarantee of human relationship. At some horrible or mundane point, we stumble. We let ourselves get in the way. We wander, and we fail."

"Well, that's great," I said.

"But it's also true you've spent an immeasurable amount of time and hope and heart wading this god awful river of doubt and absence and weather and darkness, and you've done every possible thing you can think of, all by yourself, to safeguard your last little ember of love, to keep it from snuffing all the way out."

I drew a deep breath, as though preparing for a lengthy dive, and then released it slowly.

"We all botch this thing to pieces," said Sumi. "Sometimes worse than others. But not every one of us remain nearly as committed to suturing the muddy pieces back together – owning our part."

"Maybe," I said. "Though I'm not sure it's making any difference."

"Then it isn't probably about you. Not really."

I watched her and waited.

"Most breakups," said Sumi, "I mean, they either happen or they don't. But when they comb through the woods like some kind of endless train, it usually means something else is going on."

"Like what?"

"Like I don't know," she said. "But it isn't just you holding on to that last little ember. Clare is too. In her own way."

A surge of thoughts wrapped around my head, but none found their way to their knees, much less their legs.

"A year and a half is a long time to keep a broken love forever at arm's length," said Sumi. "If you no longer want or need it. I don't think she's doing it as a charity worker."

"I don't know," I said.

"I think she's doing it because she knows what's there is real. And deep. And valuable. Maybe it got all trampled in the dirt along the way or tossed in a box and pushed into a corner or simply engulfed in the shadow of some bigger, looming giant blotting its sun. But she knows in her heart, the love you two found and explored – its bigger than all that careless mess combined. Otherwise, she would have just let go. The easier act is almost always letting go. Not hanging on."

"Does this look like hanging on to you?" I asked. "Really?"

"To her," said Sumi. "She's trying right now to hang on to her."

I nodded. "I mean, I kind of knew that, but..."

"Sometimes we cast aside every last thing surrounding us just to see our own two feet planted in the soil. Without anything else blocking the view."

I watched sparks from the fire roll into darkness.

"Love is hard," said Sumi. "But keeping ourselves together – that can be pretty impossible, too."

Close to morning following that first night of Sumi's arrival in the Scapegoat, I led her by the hand through the tall lodgepole pine all the way to the river.

"You really do this?" she asked. "Swim against this thing?"

Sumi tucked her hands beneath her arms.

"I get in and I get out," I answered. "It's not exactly swimming."

"Isn't it freezing?" she asked.

I stepped out of my clothes and walked into the river. The water's temperature bit my ankles.

"Isn't it?" she asked again, her voice barely above the roar of current.

"Oh, it's freezing," I yelled back. My teeth chattered the tempo of a novelty set of dentures. "I tell myself it's good conditioning."

"For what? A heart attack? And how do you – don't you get sucked downstream?"

"You have to use the boulders," I said. "As ballast or whatever."

I reached toward the rock-strewn shallows and then cupped my fingers over a boulder's ridge and held. My legs lifted to the surface.

On the bank, Sumi stripped down to her underwear and bra. "This is crazy," she said, and she stepped into the water. She leaned low to balance her footing on the slick river rock. "No fucking way am I doing this."

I heard a splash behind me, a squeal, and then felt her fingers wrap around my suspended ankle, felt the surge of water against my body and listened to Sumi's gasps and muttered curses. I grabbed her hand and pulled her forward, held her around her shoulders. We both laughed at the cold, waited for our bodies to adjust to it, our legs and arms suspended, our lives suddenly, maybe for the first time in this spot of the world, maybe for the first time anywhere, weightless.

When the morning sun basked the trees, Sumi's hair was still damp. She huddled near the fire, two wool blankets taught around her shoulders. She leaned into the steam from her mug of tea. I turned the coals, pushed red burls of flame beneath the two filleted trout that hissed across the cast iron.

"Just to put it out there, scout," she said. "When I stopped hearing from you and found out you headed into the woods for the summer, I mean, the whole summer, it smarted a little."

"I'm sorry," I said.

"I mean – a note, at least – that would have been nice. Especially, I don't know, after that interlude that somehow found our mouths pressed together and everything."

"Oh," I said. "*That* interlude."

"It turned out okay," Sumi said. "Gave me time to focus on my marriage. Something I was probably avoiding in the time we were spending together."

I squirted a line of olive oil across each trout fillets and turned them with the spatula. Their flesh seared against the iron.

"How is all that?" I asked. "Your marriage? Your life?"

"I'm…not sure," she said before a slurp of tea. "I'm never sure. We're talking about it. About either finding a way through or – a way out, I guess."

"Really?"

"Talking is good, right?"

"Should be," I answered. "Pretty sure I'd give my right arm to have that opportunity with Clare."

"Anyway," said Sumi. "I wanted to tell you I don't hold any grudges for your need to just walk away. I know it wasn't about me."

"It wasn't," I answered.

"But I'm really hoping we're still friends."

I looked at her – her glasses on the lower ridge of her nose, her almond eyes peering over them at me, her swollen lips.

"Of course, we are," I told her. "We never weren't."

"Good," she answered. "Good then."

"We're bonded forever in the rare art of river swimming," I added.

Sumi paused. "We'll always have Paris," she said, and beamed.

After breakfast the following morning, Sumi and I took a short hike along the ridgeline. We found an open meadow and rested our backs against the soil, closed our eyes to the cloud-withered sky.

"I should start heading out soon," she said. "I can still make it home by dinner time."

"Even sooner," I said. "Two hours hike and another two to drive."

We fell asleep in the warmth of sun. Twice I woke, watched Sumi's chest rise and fall. The treed shadows stretched across our bodies and into the surrounding pine.

When she woke, she opened her eyes and shielded them from the descending sun with her hand.

And then I told her everything. About the bears. My plan. About slowing my heart rate. About the side of the hill where I had already dug a six-foot berth. Everything.

Sumi listened silently. She nodded. For the first time in years, I didn't want to stop talking.

We ate peanut butter-slathered saltines and sliced oranges and kiwis Sumi had brought with her in her backpack. Each new wedge of kiwi I set against my tongue tasted cool and sweet.

We wandered down to the river. I lay on my back, stared up into the trees and the sunset's amber paint against them. I lowered my head into the slack water current, and Sumi lathered my hair with a bar of soap, and pressed into it until the suds disappeared from the tendrils. I sat up, and she cupped her hands in the soapy water and poured it over my head and shoulders. She bunched my hair in her hands and squeezed the water through her fingers.

We walked back along the ridgeline. The first new moon of October followed through the trees, a pale sliver high in the sky.

"You never talk about him, you know," Sumi said.

"I know."

"Wouldn't it help?"

"Would it?" I asked. "I'm not sure how."

"To keep him alive? Or to work through missing him?"

When we were young, Ben and I used to stand shoulder to shoulder on the ledge above the quarry and dare each other to dive first. I nearly always waited. I wanted to see to his flailing dive from above, his long body a contortion of legs and arms before he hit the water, the angled splash. I wanted confirmation what we were both planning was survivable. After he surfaced, he would stand on the bank dripping wet and doubled over in moaning laughter. *Then you do it!* he'd yell. *You think it's easy, you do it!*

"The thing about Ben," I said. "He was never good at standing in exactly the same spot. He just didn't have the patience or, I don't know, the attention. He was always more anxious to be in the place he was heading than the one he was standing in."

"And that makes it hard, what, to talk about him?"

"No," I said. "To remember him. To hold him in the same moment long enough to see him waiting there."

I used to imagine Ben's bones as phosphor, his energy an electric current capable of leaping through walls and rafters. In the endlessly flickering reel of home movie images in my mind, Ben was the one running across our dark lawn, the one whose face and shoulder blades blurred across screen, the shock of strawberry blond hair disappearing around a corner. He ran farther and faster than the rest of our neighborhood combined. His form was far from refined. He was gangly, awkward and impetuous. But what he lacked in style points, he made up with pure exuberance. And whatever disarray his forceful entrances and exits caused, he never once looked over his shoulder to observe or witness the falling debris.

Each time I thought of Ben, I thought two things — how in awe I was of his energy, his spirit, and how much it hurt missing knowing each other's lives, each other's hearts better. Our time together, each condensed moment was simultaneously charged and fleeting. At first intermittently, and then permanently. He was there. And then he was gone. It was the same way it always had been.

"You know those makeshift roadside memorial markers you always pass, the sides of highways?" I said. "The white crosses, sad, handwritten notes, clusters of flowers? Left for a missing loved one in the last place they drew breath? I used to wonder about those, about why people leave messages and memorials for people at the precise square foot of soil or asphalt their loved one's heart completed its final contractions. And then I realized – we leave memorials for people in the places we wish we could still reach them. If we had only arrived moments earlier. All the things we would have said."

"And what would you have said?" asked Sumi. "Had you arrived moments earlier. What would all those things be? With Ben?"

"I don't know," I said. "I'd probably ask him why he couldn't have slowed the hell down. At least on that interstate. But then, you know, you're already asking him to be someone other than the someone he was. I'd ask him to slow down for me, just five minutes, to let me catch up. I was the youngest brother. Mine were the shortest legs. And it seemed impossible, always, just to get close enough to be next to him, to gain enough distance. And then, if you did, if you made your way into one solid shared moment together...it seemed like, I don't know, he was already lurching toward the next one."

Sumi nodded, and I took a deep breath.

"We barely had time together," I told Sumi. "And now all I have is time. In front of me, and behind me, without him. Just time."

We watched a Pinyon Jay glide between trees and land on a distant conifer limb.

"You made the same mistake everybody else in the world makes," said Sumi. "You thought you had forever. And so did he."

I nodded.

"Otherwise," she said, "I think he would have slowed down long enough to let you catch up. Eventually he would have."

"Maybe," I said. "It wasn't his strong suit. But it would have been nice, at least, to find out. To have the option."

"But then you'd have the closeness to miss," said Sumi. "Instead of the wish to bridge it."

I wondered about that and stared at the ridgeline in front of us and the scudding clouds winnowed against the muted escarpment. I thought of Clare and how, with her, it was both things I missed – the closeness *and* the wish to bridge it. Both parts.

"It's exhausting," I said. "I spend half my waking hours, and half the rest, hoping to unend things that have already ended."

"Sometimes," said Sumi. "You have to let go. Of the things you can't make better. Or change."

"I've heard that," I said.

Sumi smiled.

"And anyway," I said. "How's that working for you?"

"For me?"

"Did it work for you when your life turned upside down at Oregon State, before your marriage? And then, well…your marriage?"

Sumi paused. She looked at me, her expression quizzical.

"You don't think you're running, too?" I asked.

"I could be," she said. "Or I could also be taking some time to figure out what comes next. What I want to come next."

"What do you want to come next?"

"How did this get about me?" she asked. "We were talking about you."

"Your heart is caught in a similar place. Limbo."

"Again," she said. "We were talking about you. Not me."

I nodded. "Okay, sorry."

Sumi turned to me. She scrunched her eyes against the sunlight.

"Can I ask you something?" she asked. "This is just going to shoot out my mouth, and I'll think about retracting it later, but are you worried I'm hoping for some future together, you and me?"

"Future?"

"Boyfriend, girlfriend, the whole messy ball of wax? I feel you pulling back, sometimes. You open up, and then you retreat. It makes me wonder if you aren't afraid of something. With us, I mean. With me."

She caught me off guard, and I sensed the discomfort of being cornered.

"Because I'm just trying to help, here," she said. "My shoulder is pretty much yours, absent strings."

"Okay," I said. "Good."

Sumi tilted her head.

"Wow," she said. "I mean, you said that pretty fast."

"I just mean, I don't want to be…"

"My alibi?"

"Your anything – anything in the way, I mean. That – it came out wrong."

I could see she was batting back an emotion. She turned her face from me.

"Sumi – "

"What just happened there?" she asked.

"Where?"

"I mean, do you think…? You must really think you're something," she said.

"Hardly."

"Or that I'm the kind of girl that falls head first for the first guy that tells me he wants to bury himself into the side of a mountain a month straight. *That's my demographic!*"

"Is this – are we having a fight here?"

"Oh, for Christ sake."

Sumi turned and walked the reverse direction down the trail.

"Sumi, what?"

She stopped, faced me. "No. You know what…just…I need a little time by myself, right now. You keep going. I'll meet you back there."

"Wait, Sumi – just give me – don't turn away because I'm doing a horseshit job of explaining myself all of a sudden."

"All of a sudden?"

"At all, then! Look – this matters to me. You. Us. I mean it's been the one saving grace in an otherwise awful time – the one *human* saving grace. I don't, you know, want to hurt the bears' feelings, either – if they're listening."

She pushed back a smile, raised her eyebrows and dropped her chin.

"Oh, you were doing so well, too," she said.

"Seriously, Sumi – I need this. Our friendship. It matters to me. You matter to me. But I also don't want to, I don't know, complicate anything you're trying to sort out on your own, you know?"

"And you don't think I can make up my own mind about what you may or may not be complicating?"

I watched her, silent.

"Sometimes," said Sumi, "I feel like you want me to decide – to stay in my marriage because that's the choice you wish you could make in yours."

She was right. It was the choice I wish I could make in mine – in my relationship with Clare, a choice no longer near my grasp.

"Maybe," I answered. "Maybe that's part of it. But I also, god Sumi – I'm so tired of fucking things up, you know? Every single thing around me. I don't all of a sudden want to start fucking up other peoples' things, too."

Sumi nodded. "You're kind of – I mean, you presume a lot."

I smiled. "No. Just worry a lot. Believe me, lately I've got all the grace and poise of a...Meniere's diseased Wallenda."

"A what?"

"I don't know what the fuck I'm saying, doing. Pretty much at any given time. At least around people. I just – I don't want to become any of the reasons your marriage falls apart. Isn't that okay?"

"The falling apart has already happened, Jack." Sumi's eyes teared. "You're a little late to the starting gate if you wanted a place in that relay."

"Sorry," I said. "Look, can't we – I miss the place things were with us, you and me, before the lines blurred. Can't we, can we go back to that?"

Sumi stared ahead.

"The lines are always blurred, Jack. And no – we probably can't."

I nodded, took in her response. "Can we at least – I don't want to fight. Here. With you."

"You know what, Jack?" she said. "I need a little time to myself to pull my shit together. You get that, right?"

"I do."

Sumi waited a moment and then hiked her way back down the trail.

"And Jack," she yelled, and turned one last time. "It won't work, what you are trying to do."

"I'm not – I'm not trying to do anything."

"The hibernation thing. This science experiment of yours. It won't work."

"I don't think any of us know what will or won't – "

"What you want out of it – I'm talking about what you want out of it."

I watched her.

"Your hope to avoid the pain," she said. "The not wanting to miss her. You can't burrow yourself into the side of a mountain or wait forever and hope it disappears – no matter how you try to do it, it won't work. Nothing's going to work for that, Jack."

"Okay," I said.

"It sucks," she said. "It's unfair and miserable and probably seemingly endless, but there isn't any human cure for loss, for heartbreak. None of us get a hall pass out of it. And as long as you are human, and you are human, Jack – it's going to smart like a motherfucker."

Her cheeks were wet.

"It just is," she said.

She turned and walked silently down the trail. I watched her until her form was swallowed by the darkness.

When I returned to the cabin, I felt pretty cruddy about hurting Sumi's feelings. I hadn't meant for any of that to happen. And I wondered how long she would be away, what she was thinking and whether my skills at male-female relations weren't muddled beyond repair.

Too, I felt relief. Relief at being alone enough to retrace my steps and mis-steps and the distance between them. But when she didn't return – first an hour and then two, concern took the lead again. After another hour and the slow dissolve of daylight, concern inched its way toward panic. Each moment Sumi had joined me in the Scapegoat, I had led our combined exploration. Even the weekend tracking volunteers, as familiar as they were with the same terrain, often relied on the navigation equipment Sumi lacked. I wrote a note for her and sandwiched it in the cabin door, and then headed down the trail with flashlight in hand. I hiked briskly along the ridgeline and paused every ten minutes or so to listen for sounds of movement, but all I heard was the whistle of wind through the trees.

When the first bouquet of stars pricked the sky, my heart pounded. I tried to stifle my panic with the reassurance she was likely back at the cabin already, my note unfolded on the table. I imagined her sitting by the fire, sipping tea. And that consolation would feather a good ten minutes or so against the panic, but then the fear would take over completely, with even more vigor than before. As a side effect, I found myself in the same place I had most feared for Sumi – lost. My concentration on my own movement had wavered enough I no longer knew which direction I had come from, where the main trail was or how far away. Even with my eyes fully adjusted to the darkness, I couldn't recognize the ridgeline or the talus cliffs bathed in moonlight. None of it appeared familiar.

I chose a single direction, nearly at random, and moved furtively into it – through trees and browse. Buckthorn branches slashed my cheeks. My breath grew raspy. I knew I was making a considerable mistake by giving into the panic, but it was like trying to shift the momentum while running down hill. My head down and already a ways into it, there wasn't much choice.

I tried to focus on the river below me. I watched the moonlight cascade across it. But then I imagined swallowing it. I remembered the river's cold water against my tongue and teeth, its glide down my esophagus, branching through my chest, its iced fingers reaching, easing into my stomach. It happened nearly every time I tried to swim it, a small mouthful at a time, just an accidental sip when I turned my head and gulped air, when I pulled into the current and my pectoral muscles burned like embers. I ran the wooded path, and I wondered how much of that same river I had swallowed the nights I spent swimming against it, how many cups or quarts or gallons, how much of the river was running through my own veins.

With my thoughts distracted, I forgot to watch the shifting terrain beneath my uneven gait. My left toe stubbed a lip of shale, and I stumbled. I caught my balance mid-turn only to lose it again. I flew down a slope of soil and rubble and landed like a musket ball thundered into the boulder chute. The back of my head smacked against the solid hillside and snapped my neck forward, the heel of my right foot buried beneath my butt when my body finally slowed from its meteor spiral down the mountain slope. After, all the stars were motionless. And then they blurred into one.

When I came to, the night sky was beautiful and endless. I stared into it – a soup of stars, and ignored my aching head and the contusion that felt like a hot coal expanding in girth. I knew enough not to move. Breathing was effort enough. I nodded off a time or two. I tried not to, reminded myself of the dangers of concussion-induced sleep, but there was little I could do about it. It was so much easier to let go of every last thing. Even consciousness.

It was nearly morning when I lifted myself from the tangle of brambles and duff. I moved each muscle slowly, carefully, and only winced when I bent my right knee and when I pressed against the back of my head. Everything else seemed to function, more or less. No broken bones. No torn ligaments. But when I knelt, the sky spun circles.

I let it spin until I could no longer handle it, and then I threw up.

• • • • •

The morning sky was peppered with small, feathered darts. They hovered and plummeted. When my eyes adjusted, I realized they were ravens, thick clusters, dozens strong. The sky swarmed with dark birds dipping from sky. One after the other, I watched them swoop and fall.

I walked from the base of hill where I had spent the night. I pulled myself, tree by tree, up the slope. My head pounded with each step, and my fears of intra-cerebral hemorrhage flickered between worries over where Sumi was and whether she was safe.

At the ridgeline, I could see them more clearly – the dotted plume of ravens pouring through the branches of trees. I had never seen so many birds at one time. So many birds, I thought I was dreaming them.

I moved toward them, through trees, and stepped carefully over rocks. The ravens' collective caws gained volume. They reverberated in the distance, a cacophony of excited birds.

I walked through a fire-swept side of hill, the leaning charred spires of jack pine. My hands and fingers trembled from fatigue and electrolyte depletion, and the blackened soil was crisp beneath my feet, a carpet of needles over scorched earth. The moist soil smelled of soot and smoke.

I walked through the shin-high spread of seedlings. They fluttered in the wind.

When I reached the crest of the charred hill, the raven calls were louder still. I had one more stretch of woods, spared by fire on the lee side, to move through. The air was colder there, in the shadows of Douglas fir and hemlock. I hiked slowly and braced against nearly every tree. An apron of sunlight fanned across the meadow. The ravens dipped and landed and resumed flight in twos and threes, sixes and sevens.

That's when I realized the ravens were feeding on long trenches of freshly uprooted soil. They descended on the tufts of sod, thrust their beaks into pockets of freshly liberated army cutworm moths, broke into skittering flight, circled the sky and then returned, only partially cautious of the enormous animal that unearthed their meal in the first place – the massive grizzly bear that had summoned a seemingly endless throng of dark birds from sky by ripping open the earth beneath them.

She clawed large swaths of soil from the corpse of hill in single swats. Her humped shoulders pulled divots of loam — heavy enough masses of turf and subsoil, you wondered if she wasn't on the verge of opening the entirety of the earth's contents in one sitting. Liberated pocket gophers and voles ran s-shapes towards the woods.

She had a beautiful coat of golden brown, rounded head and humped shoulders, tiny eyes, a scarred brown, wet nose. She was huge.

I knelt into the wet soil. My heart thundered.

The bear turned, lowered her gaze, and contorted her lips. She swayed her enormous head side to side, her gaze transfixed in my direction. From within the gravel beneath my knees and hands, I could feel the reverberation of her gallop. The ravens blurred. How my body folded into a perfect ball, vertebrae by vertebrae, I will never know. Only that it happened reflexively, without effort. In the oddest possible way, I felt completely calm, secure – even hopeful.

I remained still. I closed my eyes, and she paced a halo around my tucked body, first clockwise, then counter. The cold imprint of her nose pressed against my neck, then chest. She twice dipped her snout into the socket beneath my arm. Her breath was warm against my eyelids. It smelled of decayed soil and clouds. When she withdrew, she thwacked her paws against the earth near my head. She waited a moment, and then she thwacked them again. She inserted her snout once more and blew a warm slobber into my hidden face, across my lips and chin.

I didn't move. Not a millimeter. Not one breath. It was as though my body was transported a thousand miles away – across the sheet of lake ice where I first learned the secret of slowing my heart, where I initially unlocked the code. Not an artery pulsed. And then the entire world went quiet until I heard the distinctive sound of the bear moving away, heard her claws rasp against stone as she scrambled up the limestone bank and left me alone with the rolling ocean in my chest.

I yearned for Clare's hand, her warm, small fingers.

Place your hand across my chest. Press all the way against it. Feel this.

I remained still, tucked into a perfect ball. As the bear scratched her ascent, I pictured the spiral of rock and talus from her claws as aimless, falling stars.

When I opened my eyes and looked over my shoulder, I saw Sumi standing in the trees behind me and wondered if I was in the middle of a dream.

Sumi was still, seemingly conjoined with the large pine she stood beside. Her face was pointed toward me, but her eyes were expressionless. I could still feel my heart drumming the soil.

I pulled myself to my knees, and took a moment to be sure I had the stamina to get to my feet. When I did, I moved gradually toward her. I glanced over my shoulder every few steps. The coast remained clear, free of bears.

"Sumi?" I said.

Her stare held over my shoulder.

"So..." she muttered.

She told me she had observed the entire scene, had seen me moving through the woods from above, from the ridgeline where she was hiking. She had moved lower to catch up.

"And then – the bear," she said. "That was a bear, right? Or a locomotive with fur?"

"It was a grizzly. A bear."

"He thundered right below me."

"She did," I corrected.

"He's a she?"

I nodded.

"I felt like Little Red Riding Hood," said Sumi.

"That was a wolf, not a bear. Little Red Riding Hood."

"I know the difference," she said. "I mean, for a moment, everything was fairytale." She opened her grip from the tree, a finger at a time. "Only in 3D."

I smiled. "She's digging a den…her winter den. On the other side of this meadow, the lee side of this hill," I said and pointed.

"She is? Just a minute – are you okay?" Sumi's eyes locked into mine.

"Yes."

"Did she – I mean…"

"She blew snot into my face. That's it."

"Holy fuck."

I grinned so wide it hurt.

"You look like you just kissed your first girl," she said.

"In a way, I guess I did. Or her me. The crazy thing is, that's the same god damned hill I was digging *my* den."

"Bear stole your den?"

"Like a common thief."

"Difference being," said Sumi. "That one can actually survive in the thing – you should be grateful."

"Yeah," I said. "What the hell have I been doing?"

"Your head," said Sumi. She touched my neck with her hand. "It's a little…black and blue."

"I'm really sorry for hurting your feelings, upsetting you," I said.

"Most of that has very little to do with you," said Sumi. She held my arm as we climbed the bluff, partly to keep herself righted but mostly to keep me from stumbling. My mobility was about a third the strength of normal.

"Believe me," said Sumi. "My life was a mess before you got anywhere near it. It doesn't take much to scatter the ashes."

"Yeah, well," I said. "If there's one thing the two of us are short on, ashes probably isn't it."

Sumi smiled, nodded. We reached the ridgeline and paused to catch our breath.

"But I didn't mean to imply – "

"You didn't," said Sumi.

"This connection," I told her. "Our connection. It's…the one safe thing I've discovered, you know, the whole time I've been out here."

She looked at me, and smiled.

"What?" I asked.

"I mean," she said. "If you saw yourself now. Your face swollen – the contusion around your neck, the gash on your chin – "

"I get it."

"I know you mean what you're saying," she continued. "It's just that the presentation is a little…"

"Okay."

"Seriously, Jack," she said. "You look like shit right now."

"Thanks."

"Hell warmed over."

"Sumi," I said.

"Look," she said. She turned to me, and nodded reassurance. "It's okay. We're okay, here, champ. Life's complicated, but you and me – we're okay."

"I hope so," I answered.

"There's an invisible fault line – here." Sumi leaned over and ran her finger across the earth in front of our feet. "Only we can see where it is."

I smiled.

"Beyond it, the world. The whole spinning ball of monkeynaut wax. On this side, us." She waited, smiled back. "We're okay. We'll always be okay."

More than Sumi knew, I wanted that to be true.

"Thanks," I told her. My eyes welled. "I really hope so."

A southern wind sifted through the canyon that night. You could feel its moisture against your skin, its warmth. It carried the musk of creosote, the charred trees it swept past.

Sumi and I sat by our own little fire, and sipped bowls of broth. She declared the importance of my staying hydrated to ward off concussion dangers, and I complied with her advice, but the repeated servings of broth, tea and water meant continual meanders into the woods to pee, and even small hikes pretty much spit stars each time. I didn't let on how woozy I remained. It took effort to stand and then sit again.

We stared into the fire, and Sumi told me she would likely head home the following morning, if I was sure I needed to stay.

"Home, where?" I asked her.

"Missoula," she answered. "Charlie's still there. I couldn't go anywhere permanently without taking him with me. And – even if things aren't going to work out with my marriage, my husband, I'm not going to walk away without at least sorting it through. With him."

I reached for the dwindled bottle of Chartreuse nestled by the split log bench.

"Hey," she said. "Go easy on that."

"Medicinal," I said.

"Just a sip. I mean it."

I held the liquor in the back of my throat, waited through the soft burn and then swallowed. It felt immediate, a kind of reassurance. We both spotted a meteor slice the sky and stared at the space where it disappeared.

"It's good," I said. "Your plan."

Sumi looked at me. She nodded.

"You owe it to each other, and yourselves, to, you know, resolve your way to a new beginning. Or to a decision, at least. Together."

"Yep," she said. "And you?"

I looked at her, shrugged.

"I thought what happened today would change things for you," she said. "Your plans."

"I know."

"I mean, if you were hoping for some kind of sign: bear circling your body, forcing her breath into you – that one is nearly biblical."

"I guess it was."

"Pretty sure you are going to be sitting here an awful long time before a better one comes along and raps its fist across your forehead."

"A sign of what, though?"

"Absolution, maybe? How about absolution, for starters?"

"Absolution..."

"Removal of weight or sin or whatever Marvel comics monster you've had perched on your shoulder these past twenty months. Leaf through the instruction manual for Hindu mysticism, modern mythology, Tarot According to Hoyle – whatever, I'll put money down that *bear tamps earth down around your ears and walks away* is going to ring up a get out of jail free card across the gamut."

I smiled. "Tarot According to Hoyle?"

"It's huge!" said Sumi. "Today was huge. You finally have contact. More than contact – she circled your body! Twice! And then she walked away. At some point, you really do need to get on with your life, Jack. Why not now? Why not – in response to that? To her? You couldn't dream up a more perfect opening!"

"I can dream up a lot of things," I said. "That's kind of what got me into all this trouble in the first place."

"But seriously," said Sumi, "when that bear stuck her snout into your chest. I mean, all the way in. When she huffed into your face. What did you feel? Exactly then?"

"Like my heart was going to burst right out of my chest," I said. "If you and I hiked back to the spot of earth my ribcage was pressed against during that event – it would look like someone took a baseball bat to it."

"You felt afraid?"

"No!" I said. "The opposite of that. The complete opposite of that."

"What, then?"

"Alive."

Sumi smiled. She nodded. "You are, Jack. Alive. Isn't that the whole point?"

"I think it's the whole problem," I said, "more than it is the whole point."

"Jesus, Jack. You came all this way to figure something out. Or to have something proven to you. I know your heart is in pieces. It's shards and slivers and god knows what. But it's still a beating heart. It still has the stamina to get back on its feet. Because it still does when you're not looking. So why not let it? Completely, I mean. Why not let what happened today be the invitation it was – to get on with your life?"

I thought about what Sumi was suggesting, and I knew, on some level, she was asking the right question. It was the pregnant ellipsis dotting the sky. And it was also true that when that bear shoved her anvil head beneath my arm, straight into my chest, I felt the magnitude of that moment. I realized finally and completely – she exists. She's alive in the world – not just swimming around in my head. And her presence in that world is enormous. Larger than I imagined. Just like Ben's was. Just like my love with Clare was. Larger than I am. And despite the enormity and fragility of all the things I'll never tame or maybe even understand or heal from, I exist. Despite all the broken things surrounding it, my heart, when given the opportunity – or a shove from the ledge, still thumps a war dance against the bones of my chest.

But even so. In the moment it happened – wet nose pressed against my chest, and immediately after, I didn't feel reborn. Or renewed. Or re-anything. The only thing I felt – the strongest thing I felt, as soon as she stepped away – I just wanted to follow that bear wherever she was heading. I still did.

"Look," I said. "I know today – what happened today – it changes things. Maybe everything. But I still want to see if it's possible. The sleep of bears. Finding out — just finding out. I mean, that could maybe be the best last chapter to the whole rest of this."

Sumi looked away, up into the starred sky. She shook her head just enough to let me notice.

"I mean to all this," I said. "Resolution. Maybe then I'll have it. Something I can take with me. To help me adapt to – everything else."

"What you have planned," she said, "is more an epilogue — an afterword. Or an autopsy. Because that's the only *last chapter* that's going to follow your barricading yourself into the side of a frozen mountain a month straight."

"I mean," I said, "would it kill you to at least *pretend* to wonder along with me? A little, anyway?"

I didn't inform Sumi I had tried to slow my heart six times after the bear encounter, six times Sumi left me alone with enough privacy to try. Each time, I failed. My heart even sped up the last few times. I told myself the lump at the base of my neck was the cause – a temporary physical impairment. But the more Sumi tried convincing me my torpor experiment should be ditched, the more uneasy I became discussing the topic.

"I think you're looking for something that doesn't exist," said Sumi. "Resolution and heartbreak – they don't orbit the same sun."

"What else is there?" I asked. "What's left?"

Sumi looked into my eyes. She smiled. Her forehead creased between her eyebrows.

"Feeling it," she said.

I held her steady gaze.

"You don't think I'm feeling this?" I asked.

Sumi shook her head. With welled eyes, she mouthed a 'no'.

"With him, I think you did," she said. "Your brother. I think you felt every ounce of that. But with her I think you keep just enough hope along the presence of the loss to avoid having to feel the whole of it. Because the only way to feel that is to finally realize what's gone. And what can't come back."

I watched her; silent.

"I think you're afraid to feel the real loss of her," said Sumi. "And I think everything you surround yourself with – these woods, those bears... serve as protection against it."

We watched the flames eat into wood in front of us. I wished we were closer to morning and Sumi's departure. It wasn't that I was anxious to lose her company. I was tired of having to explain myself. Or fumbling for answers I knew didn't exist. And nothing, even Sumi's presence, felt that good anymore.

"She is still in Missoula," said Sumi. "In case you were wondering."

"She is."

"She hasn't gone anywhere; I see her on campus a lot. Once I saw her riding bikes with that older grad student you were so uncomfortable about, Keith Hollbeck."

"Sumi..."

It hurt. I wondered if Sumi was doing it on purpose and hoped she wasn't.

"Her hair is long, now," she said. "You both have that in common, I guess."

I was silent. I wanted Sumi to stop. My heart drummed.

"I thought you should know she's alive in the world."

"I know that," I said. "I'm aware she's alive in the world."

I held my breath, felt fortunate for the darkness and prayed to God

Sumi would stop talking.

"I wonder," she said, "how you know whether or not something has ended if neither of you has voiced it to each other. You and Clare, I mean. Does it get assumed after a matter of time?"

"Waylaid maybe," I said. "Not assumed."

"And I wonder if all the pain you're shouldering, Jack, has more to do with not knowing what's missing and what's left to mourn. It's not really that she's left you, because she hasn't told you she has. Not permanently. It's more the endless vigil you hold over the possibility she hasn't."

I pictured Clare, her hair trailing in the breeze, her beautiful, soft smile. I remembered the photograph she had given me of herself when we first started dating – Clare jumping an ocean break, her exuberant, beaming expression, her small hands aimed into clouds. I held that photograph in my fingers and knew I wanted nothing more of the world than to explore the rest of my life with her in it.

"I'm pretty sure she's left me," I said.

"But she hasn't told you that, and you haven't asked."

"No," I said.

"Maybe neither one of you has the courage to decide."

"Maybe," I said.

"Or maybe she has, and she doesn't have the courage to tell you, doesn't want to hurt you more than you've been hurt."

"I'm not sure she'd know how to get ahold of me to tell me either way."

Sumi was silent. She nodded. She wrapped her fingers, one at a time, around my forearm.

"I think that's part of it," she said. "Part of why you've lodged yourself so deep into these woods. Don't you?"

"Probably," I answered. I felt a warm welling in the center of my chest.

"Maybe you've done all this, everything you could think of to avoid letting go, to avoid her letting go. Maybe you've pushed yourself as far as you could into these woods because you already know how sad it is, how much it hurts."

I nodded. The stars blurred. I wanted her to stop talking.

"But I think this is worse, Jack. How do you know this isn't worlds worse? All this waiting? Why do you think finally hearing the word 'goodbye' from her would actually hurt worse?"

I wanted to ask Sumi how anything could hurt worse than hearing Clare voice the word goodbye, how remote the possibility I could attenuate, even a single degree, the flood of hurt that would follow. I wanted to ask her if there would even be a way to survive the impact of those seven letters, those two mated syllables from Clare's lips.

"Maybe you need to be the one to do it," she said. "Maybe you need to be the one to let go."

I shook my head.

Sumi's voice softened. She lit her hand against my face. "Here's the thing, Jack," she said. "We fall apart. Each of us. Our bodies, our lives – we're all little messes continually coming unglued, flailing our arms downstream, you know? That's all we are. But the connections we make – the truly important ones – they're stronger than that, stronger than we are. I don't think love – real love – it's not bound by the same cruddy physics, the same mortality. It's bigger than we are."

"It's bigger than we are," I answered. "But that's kind of the problem, too."

"Is it?" she asked. "I mean, for fuck sake, Jack – everything we touch falls apart when we handle it. Or it falls apart by our not handling it. Isn't it good to realize there are some things larger and stronger than we are? Things that last even after our failures at carrying them in our stupid arms? Every single thing in this universe has a manufacturer's expiration date hidden somewhere in its packaging. All of us do – everything does. The exception is love. It's the one thing that can last – can live on, even after we abandon our relationships or drop them down the stairs. Isn't it good to realize there's at least *some*thing that can do that? Even if it's the horribly lonely exception? Isn't it good to know there's one thing we can't drown? Not completely? At least, not always – not every single time?"

Sumi placed her open hand on my knee.

"Somehow, I don't know – maybe we need to measure things by how much they matter," she said. "How deep they ran and what they gave us. Not how long they last. Or lasted. Not how long we're fortunate to cradle them in our tangled arms."

I looked at Sumi's expression. She leaned close, her beautiful face, her eyes welled nearly as fully as mine.

She tilted her head toward sky. "*No matter how far we fall,*" she said, "*above our broken little heads is the widest sea of stars.* You told me that, remember? I mean, we barely matter, you know? We're here a heartbeat. You have to take the pieces of love with you you're lucky to find. Not hold forever onto the holes they leave behind."

Later, I watched Sumi's eyes until they remained closed, until I was sure she was soundly asleep, and then I got my rumpled notebook out and stared at it and at the fire hissing before me. It took me hours to figure out the exact words I needed to fill the empty page.

Sumi was right. Even if it was the one horribly lonely exception, it was reassuring to know something, one human-formed thing, could outlast the ruins of everything else that folds in our wake. It was reassuring, or it wasn't. It was, at least, possible.

Relationships come apart. Every one of them. Every bond formed is assured eventual separation. Or unraveling at their seams. Or the slow and invisible act of dissolve. But love – the fiber and lignin that joins them in the first place, its reach, its envelope — is somehow separate from the same limits of duration. Or, it can be. Of all living matter destined for finality, love is the exception — wilderness and love.

Embracing that duality: the mortality of relationship, the possible fathomlessness of love — it either brings solace or longing. Or both. But at some indeterminate point, the act of grieving, of letting go, becomes an active choice. It's what Sumi was trying to tell me. When you lose the people you love, when your path and theirs diverts, you can either wait forever in the hope they will rejoin you (or in the denial they've left at all), or you can choose the arduous journey of grieving, of missing them and learning to navigate the curve of the earth without them, of learning the impossible word "goodbye".

Those are your two choices – to remain in an endless vigil or move toward the painful letting go. It took me forever, but I finally recognized the two of them standing before me. Waiting.

When I opened my eyes, the orange wash of morning painted the treeline, and Sumi was holding my hand. She smiled.

"How are you?" she asked. She rested her fingers on my chest.

"Okay," I said. "How do I look?"

"Like you fell out of a moving car," she answered, and both of us exhaled quiet laughs.

"Oh, god, don't," I said. "Hurts."

"Okay," she said. "Okay."

She took her time placing her things in her backpack. She sipped tea and stared into the woods that had surrounded us these last several days. She never asked me again about my plans. I think she didn't want to find out I hadn't changed my mind about any of them.

"You know your way back to the trailhead?" I asked her. "The whole way?"

"I do," she said. "And I have the map."

"You know, Sumi," I said. "I couldn't head out with you now even if I wanted to. The hike, it wouldn't be safe for me right now. Like this."

Sumi was well aware of my injuries.

"I know," she said.

"I wonder...if you could do me a favor when you got back. To Missoula."

"Maybe. What?"

I handed her the folded paper from my pocket.

"Give her this?"

Sumi waited a moment and then reached her hand. She smiled.

"What's it say?" she asked.

"That I can't slow my heart anymore. That I've tried, and it doesn't work."

Sumi nodded. "That's it?" she asked.

"No," I answered. "The rest, I guess – between her and me."

Sumi nodded. "I'll get it to her," she said, and tucked the folded paper into her backpack. She inhaled a deep breath and placed the small backpack on her shoulder.

"Am I...are we going to ever see each other again?" she asked, and squinted an eye.

I waited. "Would it be easier if we didn't?" I asked.

Sumi smiled, and then she shook her head. She looked away, up into the trees. I could see her lip quiver, and she shook her head once more, faced me, and forced a smile.

I bowed my head and watched my own tears mar the soil. And then I moved toward her, pressed her body into mine. Her small fingers wrapped around the back of my neck. I tried to figure out what possible words I could string together to articulate my gratitude, my sorrow. Too, I wanted to tell her the difference she made. Not just in friendship, but in helping clear my view of the choice standing before me and in helping me see how, when finally choosing, everything would change.

Bears might be a million or more things, but monsters isn't one of them. They breathe no fire, nor do they inhale whole villages. Nor are they white fanged demons intent on violent chaos or the destruction of life. They are not nightmares.

Bears are majestic, enormously powerful, agile, mortal, mostly gentle beings moving cautiously beneath the same cold moon as we, similarly shaping a simple, hopeful path forward.

I'll never know why the army of bears walked the serrated line beside my sleep in the many days following my brother's death. Even with the benefit of time, I can't claim to have a clear perspective on the root cause, the germane purpose.

Regardless of intent, their gift, I decided, had been the simple summoning of wonder, the allure to follow something greater than myself, greater than my understanding. They brought me across the long miles of the west, deep into the woods, if only to shed light on the path through them.

In that way, each bear became a messenger. Each message, the fragmented imprint of a greater whole.

My only regret is that it took me so long to decipher the message, the truth. It took me forever to learn to read bear.

When I finally made my way through the meadow that final trek through it, the snow was so wet and thick it stuck to my eyelashes. It took me an hour to climb the steep shale opposite the ridge of South Creek, the rock beneath the snow wet and slick. With gloveless hands, I gripped the sharp ridges of the rocks, and then pulled myself up them. The sky over the Scapegoat Massif was slate.

The snow tickled my skin when it landed and melted against the back of my neck. I unzipped my jacket to my belt. The wet snow fell into the trees and whispered through crossing branches. It fell with enough volume to nearly cover my footsteps as quickly as I dented them across the trail.

When I moved to the lee side of the outcrop, I felt my heart lift, the long tailing valley beneath me stretched beneath the low, blue clouds. Snow fell in shifts across it.

When I came, finally, to the Douglas fir that marked the bear's den, I placed my fingers against its bark and leaned my body against it until

I caught my breath. Through the loam and a good half-foot of snow, I imagined the enormous animal curled into a mound somewhere beneath my feet. Her long breaths warmed the earth walls surrounding her, breath that dampened the roots of trees.

I sat at the base of the fir and waited. The moon burned through the dwindling fall of snow.

I thought of Clare and the first Christmas we shared. We were both nursing colds, had run a bath at my apartment of lemongrass and sea salt and sat together in the water, in candlelight. Clare's head rested against my chest. I wrapped my arms around her, and we simply held each other the longest time, immersed in the warm bath. We watched the mist collect against the bathroom window and run single drops that gathered momentum. They revealed a new slice of December sky and then misted over again, one by one by one.

When we rose from the bath water, we toweled each other dry and moved into bed. Our bodies steamed in the colder air of the bedroom until we tunneled beneath the covers, both of us laughing, mewing. We held each other and pressed our lips into the longest, wettest kiss.

I had never been so in love. And sometimes I wonder if connections like ours, the ones that glow brightest, aren't also the ones most impossible to sustain. They burn like meteors.

When we made love that night, my face pressed into Clare's warm neck and the wet tangles of her hair, our fingers laced with each other's, the whole world smelled of lemongrass and salt. Eyes closed, our bodies fell gently to the bottom of a warm sea, one I never wanted to leave or imagined, even, there would ever be a need to.

My wet knees against the bear's mounded den, I opened my hand against the snow and scored its surface with my splayed fingers. I wanted to go farther, and push my wrist through the delicate blanket of crystals, the pebbles and permafrost, and burrow my extended arm all the way into the moist, warm air of the bear's chamber. And maybe there, with my head and shoulders deep into snow, I could lock my elbows and pull myself forward until the soil swallowed my body whole, until I could wrap my trembling fingers around a furred wrist or padded foot and pull free one whole bear – head, teeth, fur, claws and spit from its warm nest, shucked like an wet oyster beneath the starless sky.

But none of that was possible. None of it happened. Instead, I sat in falling snow and realized I had spent an irreplaceable chunk of my life, two years and counting, locked in a futile hope to trade places with an animal whose body and breath were as separate from mine as stars and moon. I had moved my life, my heart, so far from the things that formerly grounded and held them in place, it was difficult, if not impossible, to discern my way back.

I thought of Ben, and then I wanted to reach across the final few feet of blue asphalt his car had traversed, its divots of bitumen and aggregate, across the luminous canary hash marks, through the contorted aluminum rail, past the brayed snow and earth and the beautiful nebulae of my brother's red blood across the sheared windshield. I wanted to rest my hand against Ben's, unfold a contused finger at a time, to the falling snow, open them to sky.

We fall apart.

Every living element unravels. Each breathing thing dissolves. And when they do, the ones that matter, their absence changes you. They leave you in wonder over what parts of them were true, what fragments you may have broken, and the pieces of them you'll eventually learn your way to forgetting. And the pieces you won't.

You stare into those questions, but their answers go unfielded. They become the fixed spiral of stars above your head – the permanent nexus of dust, the Large Magellanic Cloud. The most you can hope is some day you stop asking them.

I bowed my head and rocked my body back and forth. I clasped my hands. I waited for calm. It was like that for the longest while.

The snow hissed through the trees. It whistled through the fir needles and branches, its sonorous wail, and through the dead field, past brittle blades of fescue and sedges, over scorched soil, alpine bedrock and talus. It brushed my shoulders and swept gently, irreversibly into the moon-limned clouds.

Acknowledgments

Thank *you*, whoever and wherever you are, for reading this book.

I am profoundly indebted to those who've supported my writing and helped shape this novel during its lengthy, skinned-kneed journey into the world. Most prominently: Paulette Alden, Kent Nelson, Jeff Hull, Joy Tutela, and Don Pastor – **thank you.**

At least five oceans of gratitude to you, dear Nicole – for your support, understanding, humor, inspiration and love, and for your simply being in this round world to begin with. I love you.

Spiritual credit also goes to the one being in all the world at my side, and on my shoulder, from the beginning of this work – the one who gnawed the edges of the first and the endless succession of drafts, and whose beautiful, whiskered head forever presses against my chest. (Some people rescue animals; others are rescued by them.)

Finally, the bears (real and imagined). May the real ones forever remain, and cast the tallest shadows over the rest of us. As they were meant to.

About the Author

Kipp Wessel is a devoted writer, husband, father of rescued mammals, and resident troublemaker. He earned a Fiction Fellowship and his MFA from the University of Montana, and his short fiction has appeared in a dozen commercial and literary magazines. He's taught fiction writing at the University of Montana, the Loft Literary Center in Minneapolis, and regional community arts programs. This is his first novel.

More about the author at: www.kippwessel.com

CPSIA information can be obtained
at www.ICGtesting.com
Printed in the USA
BVOW04*2056010517

482802BV00003B/4/P